Also by Kathi Appelt

Keeper

The Underneath

The True Blue Scouts of Sugar Man Swamp

The True Blue Scouts of Sugar Man Swamp

Kathi Appelt

ATHENEUM BOOKS FOR YOUNG READERS
NEW YORK LONDON TORONTO SYDNEY NEW DELHI

For Dinny and Brian,
sweet as pie, wondrous as the IBWO

atheneum

ATHENEUM BOOKS FOR YOUNG READERS • An imprint of Simon & Schuster Children's Publishing Division • 1230 Avenue of the Americas, New York, New York 10020 • This book is a work of fiction. Any references to historical events, real people, or real places are used fictitiously. Other names, characters, places, and events are products of the author's imagination, and any resemblance to actual events or places or persons, living or dead, is entirely coincidental. • Copyright © 2013 by Kathi Appelt • Jacket illustration copyright © 2013 by Jennifer Bricking, • All rights reserved, including the right of reproduction in whole or in part in any form. • ATHENEUM BOOKS FOR YOUNG READERS is a registered trademark of Simon & Schuster, Inc. • Atheneum logo is a trademark of Simon & Schuster, Inc. • For information about special discounts for bulk purchases, please contact Simon & Schuster Special Sales at 1-866-506-1949 or business@simonandschuster.com. • The Simon & Schuster SpeakersBureau can bring authors to your live event. For more information or to book an event, contact the Simon & Schuster Speakers Bureau at 1-866-248-3049 or visit our website at www.simonspeakers.com. • Design by Dan Potash • The text for this book is set in Adobe Caslon Pro. • Manufactured in the United States of America • 0613 FFG • First Edition • 2 4 6 8 10 9 7 5 3 1 • Library of Congress Cataloging-in-Publication Data • Appelt, Kathi, 1954– • The true blue scouts of Sugar Man Swamp / Kathi Appelt. — 1st ed. • p. cm. • Summary: Twelve-year-old Chap Brayburn, ancient Sugar Man, and his raccoon-brother Swamp Scouts Bingo and J'miah, try to save Bayou Tourterelle from feral pigs Clydine and Buzzie, greedy Sunny Boy Beaucoup, and world-class alligator wrestler and would-be land developer Jaeger Stitch. • ISBN 978-1-4424-2105-9 • ISBN 978-1-4424-8121-3 (eBook) • [1. Swamps—Fiction. 2. Land developers—Fiction. 3. Swamp animals—Fiction. 4. Raccoons—Fiction. 5. Scouting (Youth activity)—Fiction. 6. Humorous stories.] • I. Title. • PZ7.A6455Tru 2013 • [Fic]—dc23 • 2012023723

The True Blue Scouts of Sugar Man Swamp

The First Night

1

FROM THE ROOFTOP OF INFORMATION HEADQUARTERS, Bingo and J'miah stood on their back paws and watched Little Mama and Daddy-O trundle away; their stripy gray and black silhouettes grew smaller and smaller in the deepening dusk.

Daddy-O called out, "Make us proud, boys!"

That was followed by Little Mama. "Be sure to follow orders!"

For as long as raccoons had inhabited the Sugar Man Swamp, which was eons, they had been the Official Scouts, ordained by the Sugar Man himself back in the year Aught One, also known as the Beginning of Time. Of course, Bingo and J'miah would follow the orders. They knew them by heart.

OFFICIAL SUGAR MAN SWAMP SCOUT ORDERS
- keep your eyes open
- keep your ears to the ground
- keep your nose in the air

- be true and faithful to each other
- in short, be good

These orders were practical, and the raccoon brothers had no problem following them. Besides, Bingo and J'miah weren't *ordinary* Swamp Scouts. They were, in fact, Information Officers, a highly specialized branch of the Scout system. And because of this there were two additional orders:

- always heed the Voice of Intelligence, and
- in the event of an emergency, *wake up the Sugar Man*

The first additional order was easy enough, as we shall soon see, but the second was a different matter. The problem? Nobody really knew exactly where the Sugar Man slept, only that it was somewhere in the deepest, darkest part of the swamp. He hadn't been seen in many years.

The bigger problem? Waking the Sugar Man up wasn't all that easy. He slept like a log. Literally.

The biggest problem? What if he woke up cranky? Every denizen in the swamp knew that the *wrath of the Sugar Man* was something to avoid.

He also had a rattlesnake pet, Gertrude.

Crotalus horridus GIGANTICUS (also known as CHG).

Brothers and sisters, the stakes were high.

2

GOT TO GO WAY, WAY BACK INTO YESTERDAY AND THE yesterday before that, maybe a million yesterdays, actually more than a million, a *gazillion* yesterdays, to hear about the Sugar Man. Got to go back to when the sea had only barely rolled its way south into the Gulf of Mexico and left behind the slow-moving Bayou Tourterelle, which meandered through the middle of a wide, open marsh.

Sitting as it was in the deep southern side of the continent, the marsh had long days of sunshine and plenty of rain, all the right ingredients to give birth to a whole host of species of plants and animals. And like a tree rising up out of the rich red dirt, soon enough a creature born of the swamp rose up too.

He was taller than his cousin Sasquatch. Taller than Barmanou. Way taller than the Yeti. His legs and arms were like the new cedar trees that were taking root all around, tough and sinuous. His hands were as wide and big as palmetto ferns. His hair looked just like the Spanish moss that hung on the north side of the cypress trees, and the rest of his body was covered in rough black fur, like the fur of the *ursus americanus luteolus*, UAL, also known as Louisiana black bear, that had taken up residence in the area.

You could say that he was made up of bits and pieces of every living creature in the swamp, every duck, fox, lizard, and catfish, every pitcher plant, muskrat, and termite.

Of course, Bingo and J'miah knew the history. Little Mama and Daddy-O had made sure of it.

Over the years, however, the Sugar Man has grown older and older and sleepier and sleepier. Let's not forget that he's been there for too many years to count, since back before we even measured time in years. But just because the Sugar Man is old and sleepy doesn't mean he can't spin an alligator over his head and toss him into orbit. Nosirree, Bob. In fact, whenever he gets mad, he tends to throw things.

All in all, it's not a good idea to stir up the *wrath of the Sugar Man.*

3

But right then, the Sugar Man was not on the minds of Bingo and J'miah. Standing there, on the rooftop of Information Headquarters, they watched their parents' shadows fade into the thick woods of the swamp. Bingo straightened up as tall as he could and saluted. But when he turned toward his brother, he could see that J'miah was on the verge of sniffles. Sniffles, especially brother-sniffles, are highly contagious. Bingo did *not* want to sniffle. He pinched his nose to keep the sniffles from welling up. He was not going to sniffle. No way, José. Not this big boy.

He knew that he would miss Little Mama and Daddy-O. In fact, he already did. But the missing part was not as strong as the excitement part. He blew his nose as hard as he could.

"We're official," he said, and he slapped his brother on the back, then did a little two-step atop the DeSoto.

You heard me. The DeSoto.

4

BACK IN 1928, WALTER P. CHRYSLER INTRODUCED HIS
newest car. The DeSoto. It was named for the Spanish
conquistador, Hernando de Soto. It was *la-di-da-di-da*. In
the first twelve months of production DeSoto set a record:
81,065 cars. More than Pontiac. More than Buick. More
than Graham-Paige.

You weren't anybody unless you had a DeSoto.

Nowadays, there are only a few DeSotos in existence.
Some of them are parked in forgotten garages, waiting for
their drivers to remember them. Some of them have been
lovingly restored and their owners proudly show them off
in Fourth of July parades and things like that. Most of
them, sadly, have been relegated to junkyards or left to rust
in overgrown pastures. All in all, they're hard to find.

But one of them, a 1949 Sportsman, has been sitting
atop a little knoll along the banks of the Bayou Tourterelle
for more than sixty years, looking out over the water.

And in all that time, the old Sportsman has not budged,

not an inch to the east, not an inch to the west. Its once-shiny green paint has turned into a veneer of dusty red rust, and its hood ornament, a bust of the old explorer Hernando de Soto, stares straight ahead. For many years the car sat there, all sealed up and empty, sinking into the damp red dirt a little bit more each year. And at the same time, the prodigious vines and ferns that thrived in the boggy swamp crept up its sides and top until it was pretty much completely hidden.

Lots of critters walked right by it—some even walked over it—and did not even notice it. The dusty red rust with its flecks of green paint were so close to the color of the dirt and the vines that it became camouflaged. Even human-types who paddled their pirogues up the Bayou Tourterelle missed it entirely.

If you did happen to stumble upon it and looked at it head-on, you might think that it was just a ghost of a car, and that your eyes were playing tricks on you. A car, after all, is meant to move, not hide all alone beneath the dirt and shrubs. And the sad truth is that it could have just slid right into the bayou of its own accord, that's how lonely it was . . . and it might have . . . it came close a few times . . . except for the raccoons.

Raccoons can make a cozy nest just about anywhere. They will set up housekeeping in underground burrows, abandoned outhouses, unused chimneys, garbage cans, tree cavities, old cisterns—the list is endless.

You wouldn't think that an abandoned DeSoto would be one of those places, but thanks to the wet ground beneath it, eventually a small hole in the floorboard on the passenger's side rusted through, making an entryway.

And soon enough, a stripy pair of raccoons discovered that open hole and made themselves right at home. It was a perfect place to settle in and raise their kits, and that's what they did. That original pair of raccoons turned out to be the great-great-greater-greatest-grandparents of Bingo and J'miah.

The old car could have simply been a raccoon nursery for generations of our *procyonid* crew, it was cozy enough, but one night a random strike of lightning hit so close that every inch of fur on the raccoons' bodies poofed straight out. They watched as all the numbers and dials on the dashboard lit up. The raccoons could also see that the hood ornament cast an eerie orange glow, like a faded firefly. It was a historic moment, especially because that was when they first heard the all-important Voice of Intelligence. It came from the direction of the dashboard, more specifically through the radio, and floated atop the invisible sound waves inside the car. "Prepare for rain," it said. And sure enough, it started to rain. Ever since then the

5

CHAP BRAYBURN, ONE OF THE FEW MEMBERS OF THE local *Homo sapiens*, on the other hand, did tell a lie. When his mother asked him if he was okay, he said, "Yep." But he knew that wasn't true. Ever since his grandpa Audie Brayburn passed away just a few days ago, nothing was okay. When you are twelve, and the very best grandpa in the world, the person who taught you more than anyone else, including your mother, walks into a grove of cypress trees, curls up in the arms of their massive roots, and just flat-out dies? Without even saying good-bye? That was not okay.

Moreover, Grandpa Audie died just when it seemed like all heck was breaking loose. Instead of sticking around, "Audie went to meet his maker" as Brother Hadley at the Little Church on the Bayou kept saying, over and over.

Everyone at the funeral told Chap, "You're the man of the household now, son." Chap wasn't sure he was done being a boy yet. Nevertheless, when he looked at his mother, with her crestfallen face, he knew he was going to have to man

DeSoto has been Information Headquarters for the Sugar Man Swamp Scouts, most recently Bingo and J'miah—Information Officers.

The Voice has never told a lie. Not once.

up, especially now that their landlord and the official owner of the entire Sugar Man Swamp, Sonny Boy Beaucoup, had unceremoniously raised the rent on their combination home and café, their only source of lodging and income.

It wasn't just a small amount of cash that Sonny Boy demanded. It was a boatload.

"We might have to leave," said his mother when she got the notice.

Leave? Leave the swamp, with its ancient trees, with its thick and winding Bayou Tourterelle, with its millions of insects and brilliant green peepers? Leave all of that? Thinking about it made Chap's throat burn, as if there were a box of matches all lit up back there. He was definitely not okay. He tried swallowing to put out the fire. But it didn't help.

And what about the ivory-billed woodpecker? Chap knew that only a few people in the entire world still believed that the ivory-bill, or IBWO, still existed, particularly in the Sugar Man Swamp. But Grandpa Audie had assured Chap that it was still out there. "I even took a photo of it," Audie told him, "a one-of-a-kind Polaroid." Then he followed with, "Some time back," which Chap understood was 1949. More than sixty years ago.

In his hands, Chap now held his grandfather's old birder sketchbook. After Audie had lost his Polaroid one-of-a-kind photo, he never took another photograph of anything. Instead he turned to drawing. In the sketchbook, there were rough pictures of every kind of bird that Audie had ever seen. Curiously, there was no sketch of the ivory-bill, despite Audie's claim of catching it on the photo. Audie had declared, "I'll draw it when I see it again." Then he added, "As long as the swamp is here, the bird could return." So there was an empty white page, smack in the middle of the book, waiting for that drawing. Waiting for that bird.

Chap brushed the leather cover with his palm and pulled it toward his face. It smelled like raw sugarcane and bullfrogs and red dirt. It smelled like Grandpa Audie. The heat in Chap's throat grew.

Then he opened the sketchbook and flipped quickly through the pages of Audie's drawings. None of them were perfect, not at all "museum quality" as Audie would say, and on each one he had added something funny, like the diamond ring he drew around the leg of the brown thrasher, and the little hat he put on the red-winged blackbird.

He told Chap that the brown thrasher was so plain, "It needed some jazzin' up." And the red-winged blackbird was dapper, so of course, "He has to have a hat." That was Audie. But even though Audie added his own quirky elements, he still managed to capture the nature of every bird he drew.

No one, thought Chap, loved birds more than Grandpa Audie. He stared at the blank page, the one that was supposed to hold the ivory-billed woodpecker. IBWO.

"We're going to find it, old Chap!" his grandpa had said over and over. But now? Now that Audie was gone? The page was so empty, Chap had to close the book fast. His throat ached.

To make matters worse, he heard his mother call from her room, *"Nosotros somos paisanos."*

Chap didn't expect that. It was his grandfather's special message, just between them, the message that his grandfather had told him every night before bed. It had to do with his name, Chaparral, another name for the greater roadrunner. Most birds have a legend attached to them, and the one for the chaparral was that he was true and faithful. A fellow countryman. A *paisano*.

Audie's sketch of the greater roadrunner included a large heart in the center of its breast, a heart that he had added on the day Chap was born. And right at the bottom of the page, Chap could see where his grandfather had erased the word "roadrunner" and written "Chaparral" over it, so that the name said "Greater Chaparral."

Nosotros somos paisanos. We are fellow countrymen. We come from the same soil. That's what it meant. Grandpa Audie had said it to him every single night of his life. Chap

15

knew that his mother meant well by saying it, but instead of comforting him it just made a big cloud of lonesome hover above his head. He closed his eyes, and if it hadn't been for his cat, Sweetums, who at that very moment jumped onto his bed and startled him, he knew that he might've burst into tears. How manly would that be?

6

ONE OF THE JOBS OF THE SUGAR MAN SWAMP SCOUTS is to go on missions. Now that his parents had both been gone for at least an hour, Bingo was bored. It was way past time for a mission. From his perch on the front seat of the DeSoto, he looked into the rearview mirror above the dash, brushed his fur back, took a good long look at his handsome black-and-white mask and his pointy little ears, and said, "J'miah?"

He only barely heard his brother's reply, "Mmmm?"

J'miah was digging out some old junk that had gotten stuck in the crack between the backseat and the seat's back, tossing it onto the floorboard behind the passenger's seat.

Bingo just said two words: "Mission Longleaf." He waited. There was silence. He waited another minute.

More silence.

Finally, Bingo saw J'miah's head pop up. His black eyes glowed in the darkness. His black mask was a carbon copy of Bingo's own black mask. In fact, to an onlooker they appeared almost exactly alike, except that Bingo had a little tuft of fur that sat straight up between his ears. It was a source of some consternation for Bingo. He was constantly slicking it back. Alas, there was no taming it.

But back to the mission . . . While J'miah's eyes glowed, Bingo announced, "I'm going to climb the longleaf pine."

That got J'miah's attention. "Why?" he asked.

Bingo sat up straight. "Because Scouts need a mission!" He looked back at J'miah. He could practically see J'miah's invisible thinking cap. Bingo also knew that underneath that cap J'miah was thinking about Great-Uncle Banjo.

Everyone in the swamp knew the sad fate of Great-Uncle Banjo. The old Scout was legendary for his ability to climb to the very tops of the highest trees. He'd climb so high that you couldn't even see him from the forest floor. The only way that the rest of the critters knew he was up there was from the birds' reports. They flew by, and he waved to them. Then they flittered down to the ground and told everyone how high up he was.

"At least a hundred feet," a robin declared.

"More like a hundred and twenty," the red-tailed hawk said.

"Wow," responded the critters below.

Problem was, Great-Uncle Banjo was a dead legend. Not a living legend. One day he climbed into the top of the old loblolly, only to be caught in a wind shear from a humongous thunderstorm. Before he could shimmy down, the top of the tree cracked off and came tumbling to the ground, Great-Uncle and all.

It was a sorry end to a fabulous story.

Little Mama had recounted this tragic tale to the brothers numerous times. Now Bingo looked over the seat at J'miah. Yep, sure enough, J'miah's invisible cap was pressing down on his eyebrows, making him squint. And that, all by itself, served to heighten Bingo's resolve.

J'miah said, "I don't think that's practical."

Bingo *knew* J'miah was going to say that. He just knew it. J'miah was always being practical, just like Little Mama. But Bingo was done with practical. He was much more like Daddy-O, who had always been good for some sort of falderal. And in Bingo's heart of hearts he also knew he had inherited Great-Uncle Banjo's special trait, which when analyzed meant: Born. To. Climb.

Besides, without a mission, how could they call themselves bona fide Sugar Man Swamp Scouts?

As if J'miah could read Bingo's thoughts, he added, "I'm on a mission already. It's called Mission Clean-Up Headquarters."

Bingo slapped his forehead with his paws. "That's not a mission. That's a chore."

"But there's all kinds of stuff back—" J'miah started to say. Bingo interrupted him.

"J'miah," he said. "I just know there's something at the top of that pine tree that I'm supposed to see." His paws were calling to him: *Climb! Climb!*

"What?" J'miah asked. "What could be at the top of the longleaf pine tree except for long leaves?"

That was a good question. What was up there? Bingo felt the tuft between his ears pop up. But he also felt the tingling in his paws.

"We won't know until the mission is complete," Bingo said.

J'miah scratched his left ear. Bingo had a point. Then a shiver ran up his back. He hoped that Bingo didn't notice, because if there was one thing J'miah was not proud of, it was the fact that he hated to climb.

Okay, let's just be honest here. J'miah was terrified of heights. He knew it was deeper than the knowledge of Great-Uncle Banjo. And it scared him even more to think about his brother climbing all the way to the top of the longleaf pine, the tallest tree in the forest. It made him queasy . . . like he-might-throw-up queasy . . . that kind of queasy.

He glared at Bingo with his hardest squint. Sometimes, he knew, squinting worked in his favor. But tonight, their first night on duty without Little Mama and Daddy-O, Bingo seemed determined to climb that tree.

7

Kint kint kint kaPOW.

If you ever did hear an ivory-billed woodpecker, that is the sound it would make.

Chichichichi.

If you hear that sound, turn around and run.

Canebrake rattlesnakes.

Chichichichi.

8

EVERYONE KNOWS THAT RACCOONS ARE FAIR CLIMBERS. It's not unusual to see them perched on a branch some twenty or thirty feet up or more, but higher than that, and Houston, we've got a problem. Unlike squirrels, who are compact and have flaps underneath their armpits that help them glide, raccoons are a bit on the bottom-heavy side, so if they get too high up in a tree, well, the tree tends to bend in a downward motion. So let's just say that they *usually* don't get too high up in a tree.

Most raccoons don't, at any rate.

But Bingo was not most raccoons. He could feel it in his paws. When he held them in front of his masked face, they started to itch. Itching. To. Climb. Which was what he planned to do. Straightaway.

"It's my mission," he said.

Mission Longleaf.

J'miah could stay in the DeSoto and continue cleaning the backseat, but not Bingo. He had a tree to climb.

Go, Bingo!

"I'm leaving," he said. J'miah did not respond. Bingo waited. It only seemed fair to give his brother a chance to come along.

J'miah pulled his invisible thinking hat down hard. He didn't say anything. Not one single thing.

"Yep," Bingo said. "I'm really going."

Squint.

Then Bingo eased his way toward the exit on the passenger side of the car. He looked back over his shoulder.

Squint.

"Bye." He waved.

Squint. Squint. Squint.

J'miah squinted so hard, his eyes were just tiny slits. He and Bingo were a pair. A duet. Brothers. The order was to be true and faithful to each other. Could J'miah let Bingo go on a mission alone?

Arrrggghhhh! he wanted to scream.

But just as Bingo slid into the exit hole, they both heard these unmistakable sounds: *split splat sploot* . . . RAIN!

And before they could even blink, here it came, pouring down. Then . . .

ZZZTTTTT! . . . . A bright bolt of lightning zipped out of the sky and struck so close to the old car that the electricity made their fur stand straight up.

"That was close!" said Bingo.

"Do you think it was close enough?" asked J'miah.

"If we're lucky!"

They didn't have to wait. Sure enough, the big bolt of lightning hit so close to the DeSoto that the old battery got a big, fat charge, which in turn shot through the rusted wires and switches and tubes and *zzzttt!* A pale purple light lit up the dashboard.

"Information!" the Scouts said together.

J'miah abandoned his clean-up mission, scrambled into the front seat, and sat next to Bingo. "Get ready," he said.

Bingo grabbed the steering wheel with both paws. The numbers on the dash glowed in the darkness. And then . . . *ssssttt . . . blip blip bloop . . . oooowwwwweeee* . . . a voice, a deep, loud, clear voice, the Voice of Intelligence, floated atop the airwaves. ". . . it might be raining now, but be prepared for clear skies, with a few clouds . . ." And then, as quickly as it came, it faded away, along with the purple numbers.

"Roger," said Bingo.

"Roger," echoed J'miah.

They both saluted. As brand-new Information Officers, they had just followed Special Order Number One: Always heed the Voice of Intelligence. The Voice hung in the air. It wasn't a scary voice. It was simply the one that occasionally slipped out of the dashboard, always after a bolt of lightning struck nearby.

Of course, in this early summertime of the year, thunderstorms in the swamp were frequent, practically nightly. And while our Scouts probably didn't know it, the metal from the DeSoto seemed to attract more than its fair share of proximal lightning strikes. After all, aside from the aluminum cans that floated down the bayou from irresponsible campers, what other metal structures were there in the Sugar Man Swamp?

It took a while for the storm to abate, but as the raindrops died down and stopped their relentless beating on the roof of the car, Bingo peered at the now-dark dashboard with its dials and buttons. He rested his paws on the old steering wheel and then scratched his right ear. There was nothing of note in the Intelligence Report that they had just received. It was pretty standard stuff, a little rain, a few clouds. It hardly seemed worth broadcasting. *Be prepared for clear skies, with a few clouds.* Easy peasy. Clear skies were easy to prepare for.

But first, Bingo had a tree to climb. And despite his invisible thinking cap, J'miah said, "I'm coming too."

Bingo's tuft stood straight up. He grinned.

"Well," said J'miah, wishing that someone had caught Great-Uncle Banjo. "Someone has to catch you if you fall."

Bingo had no intentions of falling. There was something in the top of that tree that he had to see. He was certain of it. He was a Scout on a mission. Mission Longleaf.

9

THE DESOTO ACTUALLY *WASN'T* THE ONLY METAL structure in the swamp. Aside from the aforementioned soda and beer cans, there was a small building a mile or so north, a wooden building with a wide front porch that faced the road, a road known as the Beaten Track. The building had a screened-in back porch that faced the bayou, and a tin roof, a roof that might have attracted the occasional bolt of lightning but for the lightning rods that thwarted their strikes.

On the front side of the building was Paradise Pies Café. The backside of the building was the home of the newly deceased Audie Brayburn, proprietor of Paradise Pies Café, along with his daughter and his grandson, Chap.

As Chap sat there in his bedroom, he looked up at the ceiling fan as it slowly spun in circles over his bed, and tried to remember everything his grandfather had told him about the ivory-billed woodpecker. He knew the bird was the reason Audie had come to the swamp in the first place. It was also the reason Audie had stayed. Why was Audie so sure that the bird might be there?

"I took a photo of it," he had told Chap.

If only, thought Chap, I had that one-of-a-kind photo.

"It's in the DeSoto," Audie had told him, which was no help at all. Every time they went on one of their ramblings through the swamp, which was almost every day, they kept a lookout for the old car. Sometimes they went by foot. Sometimes they took the pirogue and pushed their way back and forth along the Bayou Tourterelle.

It was on one of those ramblings that Audie told Chap that he had met the Sugar Man, right on the banks of the Bayou Tourterelle.

"Grandpa," Chap had said. Chap knew that it was one thing to believe his grandfather about the woodpecker. It was another to believe him about the Sugar Man.

Nevertheless, Audie had talked about both the woodpecker and the Sugar Man with such certainty that Chap couldn't help but believe him. After all, Audie had never lied to him. Or at least Chap didn't think he had.

The thing is, even though Audie told others about the woodpecker, he never spoke to anyone but Chap about the Sugar Man. Chap knew why.

"If the outside world thought they could find the Sugar Man, why, they'd swarm all over this place, trying to hunt him down," Audie had told Chap. "They'd be tramping and stamping and shooting at every shadow they saw. Heck, they'd probably shoot each other."

Which raised the question, "Wouldn't they also swarm this place looking for the woodpecker?" Chap wanted to know.

Audie paused, then said, "Yep, but it would be different. . . . Instead of a swarm of honeybees, it'd be a swarm of hornets."

For example, according to Audie, there was one time, way back when, that a posse of folks got all riled up and determined to capture the Sugar Man.

Seems that someone from the East Coast had told them all about the Wendigo, and it rattled that posse. The Wendigo is mean and nasty, so they just assumed that the Sugar Man was mean and nasty too, even though there was no connection at all between the Wendigo and the Sugar Man. All they knew was that the Sugar Man should be exterminated.

So, they came riding through the swamp on their tall horses, with their ropes and axes and shotguns. For days, they roped and hacked and shot at things. After a while they got tired of riding around in the swamp all day on sweaty horses, especially with all those mosquitoes and pricker vines. So they finally gave up, but not before they tramped over rabbit warrens, sliced down old vines, stomped on quails' nests, and generally made a big mess of things.

They never saw a single trace of the Sugar Man. "But what if they had?" Audie had asked. Chap considered their ropes and axes and shotguns. It didn't take him long to see the picture. Hornets. A whole swarm of them.

How, wondered Chap, could the Sugar Man Swamp be the Sugar Man Swamp without the Sugar Man?

Chap sucked in a deep breath. He looked at the tall trees all around him, their branches draped with lacy moss. He took in the baby teals riding behind their mama on the slow current of the bayou. He gazed at the deep, deep green of the wispy willow branches as they dipped their fingers into the water.

"This is paradise, old Chap," Grandpa Audie had said, spreading his arms out wide.

"And we come from the same soil," Chap had added. Then he held his own arms out. He stretched them as wide as he could, as if he could hold the entire swamp in between them.

Now, outside Chap's window, the rain eased up. *The same soil.* His grandfather's voice slipped through his head, *Nosotros somos paisanos.*

He rubbed the edges of the old sketchbook between his

fingers again. The cloud of lonesome puffed up. The swamp was called the Sugar Man Swamp, but it could have been named for his grandfather—the Audie Brayburn Swamp. That's how much Grandpa Audie had loved it.

Chap loved it too.

The same soil.

Home.

10

THE TROUBLE WAS, HOME OFFICIALLY BELONGED TO Sonny Boy Beaucoup, who wanted a whole boatload of cash, *or else.*

Or-else-or-else-or-else. Such small, mean, nasty words. Two little words. Chap knew exactly what they meant: *paradise lost.*

"No," he said. It was true what all those folks at the funeral had told him. Without his grandpa, it was Chap's turn to be the man of the household. Yep. He'd figure out a way to load that boat with cash. He would. With that, the heat in his throat cooled down a bit and he managed to swallow the last of it in one big gulp. A clean, cool breeze pushed its way through his open window.

As he drifted off to sleep, he didn't notice the odd *rumble-rumble-rumble-rumble* in the distance.

Sweetums did, however. The big ginger cat curled his tail as tightly around his face as he could and closed his eyes.

That was no ordinary rumble. Tomorrow he would have to warn his people, a task that would be made more difficult by their persistent unwillingness to learn Catalian.

11

As soon as the rain stopped, our two Scouts squeezed out the entryway on the passenger side of the DeSoto and took a big, deep breath of the midnight air. It was still humid, but the rain had passed and the sky was clear . . . except for the occasional cloud that drifted by. It was just like the Voice of Intelligence had said: *Be prepared for clear skies, with a few clouds.* That's exactly what Bingo and J'miah saw through the branches of the thick trees. It was what they were prepared for, so they were not surprised.

In that bright new moment of the night, Bingo had one thing on his mind, one singular sensation: climb.

J'miah had one thing on his mind too: prevent Bingo from meeting the same fate as Great-Uncle Banjo. It was an unsettling thought, one that made him imagine two different options. The first option was to climb up after Bingo. With a shiver, he quickly erased that thought out of his mind.

But the second option was almost as bad: to stand at the

bottom of the tree and catch Bingo if he fell. That gave J'miah a vision of two flattened raccoons. Rather like a stack of stripy pancakes, without the butter and syrup.

Then it occurred to him that he had a third option. He would just pull his invisible thinking cap so far over his eyes that he would not be able to see Bingo's death-defying climb at all. That way, if his brother fell, J'miah would be spared the horror of witnessing it, and also would not be forced to try to save him. Although he had to admit that it was a somewhat cowardly option, it seemed like the most reasonable course of action.

Sadly, none of J'miah's thoughts slowed Bingo down.

When they reached the longleaf pine tree, Bingo gave J'miah a pat on the head. "Wait here and watch," he said, and without even hesitating, up he went. Just like that. Ten feet. Twenty feet. Thirty feet. His stripy backside was on the up and up.

The higher Bingo went, the better he felt. Ahh, he thought, this is what I was meant to do—climb! He put his nose in the air. Gone was the smell of mud and decaying leaves, the common smell of the forest floor. Instead, here was a new smell, the smell of fresh pine, clean and crisp and cool. He took a deep breath. Oh, happy night! This was not at all like the dark, stuffy interior of Information Headquarters. Not. At. All. He kept going.

But just as he began his final ascent, the breeze bleeeewwww . . . the tree swwwwaaaayyyed . . . the branches creeeeeeaaaakkked.

"Whoa," he cried. He wrapped all four paws around the trunk.

"Bingo?" J'miah's voice climbed up after Bingo.

Bingo could hear his brother's worry. He gripped a little harder. He refused to look down, and instead looked up. There was the beckoning top. He was so close, only a dozen more feet. He reckoned he could scurry up there for a quick look and then hurry down.

He heard J'miah call again, "Bingo!" J'miah's voice was worrieder than ever. Up? Down? Up? Down?

"Bingo?"

Before he could make a choice, Bingo put his stripy bottom in gear and went for it . . . up . . . Up . . . UP. . . . He went right to the very tip-top!

Victory! It was glory hallelujah, get out the biscuits, my-oh-my-oh-my. Bingo reveled at the grandeur all around him. He had never looked down at the tops of trees before. He had only ever looked up through their branches. Now he could see miles and miles of treetops, dark gray shadows in the deep blue night. What a glorious sight.

In the starlight he could also see the sparkly water of the

Bayou Tourterelle beneath him. It had never looked more beautiful, like a silver ribbon running in curves.

He leaned back, his face turned up. Just above his head were stars galore. So many stars! They streamed across the sky, just like the bayou streamed below. And every single one of those stars was white . . . except for the one that blinked, which was *red*.

Hmmm, he thought. No one had ever told him about a red star. Then it occurred to him that maybe, just maybe, that was what he was supposed to find. Of course!

"I've made a discovery!" he shouted down to J'miah. "A red star! A blinking red star!"

J'miah called up, "What does it look like?"

"A blinking red star?" said Bingo. He thought about saying "Duh," but he was too dazzled by the sight of it to be grumpy. Instead, he thought of two words: *wowie zowie!*

This was major. Nobody in the history of the Sugar Man Swamp Scouts had ever reported the discovery of a blinking red star. Then he thought, Hey, explorers get to name their discoveries, don't they?

But what does one name a red star that blinks?

He stared at the star, blinking on and off. When he looked up at the other stars, they were all so far away, but his red star seemed so close, as if it had been waiting for him, Bingo, to discover it.

It was, he decided, his special star, and it deserved a special name. The only star name he had ever heard was Twinkle. Back when he was just a kit, Daddy-O had sung a song to him about a little star named Twinkle.

No.

This was a red star and it blinked.

All at once, he knew the perfect name. "I'm going to name you Blinkle," he announced. Rhymes with "twinkle." Nobody ever said raccoons weren't clever.

12

CLEVER COULD APPLY TO SOMEONE ELSE, TOO, NAMELY
the World Champion Gator Wrestler of the Northern Hemisphere. Jaeger Stitch knew exactly what she wanted. Fame
and fortune. She wanted it in spades.

And she knew exactly how to get it: by turning the Sugar
Man Swamp into the Gator World Wrestling Arena and
Theme Park. It would require taking down several hundred old trees to clear the space for the stadium. She would
also need to fill in at least two thousand acres of marsh
to make a parking lot for the millions of people who she
knew were clamoring to see her mighty-mighty self.

Shoot, she was already in negotiations for a reality television show and everything.

Was there even one tiny shred of decency in Jaeger Stitch?
Well, she did appreciate the swamp for being a nursery for
baby gators. Then again, why would she need a natural
nursery when she could just raise the little hatchlings herself in the swimming pool that she planned to install? She

could charge extra for letting people swim with the baby gators. Heck, she could charge even more for letting them swim with their mamas. Besides, what were old dead trees and mucky marsh worth to anyone?

Her point exactly.

So really, if you thought about it, maybe there wasn't so much decency in Jaeger Stitch. "Clever" might be the wrong word too.

Let's use "driven." That seems more apt.

13

BUT HOW, YOU MIGHT ASK, COULD JAEGER STITCH GET her greedy little hands on an entire swath of prime swamp? Answer: by getting her greedy little hands on Sonny Boy Beaucoup.

The Beaucoup Corporation had owned the swamp for, like, three hundred and fifty years, even before the French government sold it to the U.S. government back in Thomas Jefferson's day in a little transaction called the Louisiana Purchase. As part of the deal, a crafty pirate named Alouicious Beaucoup bought the swampland for a song. The confusing waterways and the massive cypress groves of the Bayou Tourterelle provided the ideal hideout for his enterprising gang of buccaneers.

Of course, the Sugar Man was completely aware of Alouicious. After all, he received regular reports about the pirates from his trusty Scouts. To the Sugar Man, the pirates didn't seem to be doing any harm to his beloved swamp. Plus, they seemed to keep the alligator population in check with their frequent alligator roasts, a point that his pet rattlesnake, Gertrude, CHG, appreciated on behalf of her fellow rattlers, which alligators have been known to eat from time to time. Moreover, the pirates weren't trying to hunt the Sugar Man down with their pesky cannons and muskets, or poke him with their little swords.

But then came the chantey. Pirates were all about chanteys. They had a chantey for raising the mast. They had one for lowering the mast. They had one for swabbing the deck, several about drinking grog, and more than a few about lost loves.

But one day they began to sing a new chantey that absolutely grated on the Sugar Man's nerves. You know how it is when a song gets played over and over and over until you can't get it out of your head? And no matter what you do, the song just keeps repeating itself until you think you're going to go bonkers?

Yep. The song, which we won't repeat here because we don't want anyone going bonkers, made the Sugar Man crazy. He couldn't sleep, he couldn't concentrate, he couldn't get the darned thing out of his head. And it didn't help that just when he thought he might get some peace from it, the pirates cranked it back up again. They even added accompaniment on the concertina, an instrument that annoys even in the best of circumstances.

Finally, the Sugar Man couldn't stand it any longer. He stomped through the swamp until he reached the pirate hangout, and grabbed several Chanteymen at once, swung them over his head, and flung them far and wide. Some landed in the tops of trees, some landed on the backs of alligators, and some landed in the Gulf of Mexico.

The rest of the crew abandoned ship, so terrified were they of the creature as tall as a tree, with hands as wide as palmettos. Alouicious was left alone, his heart pounding faster than the flapping fins of flying fishes.

The captain fell to his knees and begged for mercy!

Seeing his obvious advantage, the Sugar Man struck a deal, which he made Alouicious write down, using the captain's own blood as ink.

A deal —I, Alouicious Beaucoup, and all of my heirs hereafter, solemnly promise to protect the swamp, and all of its critters, forever, or else risk the wrath of the Sugar Man.
        Signed, A. Beaucoup

P. S. Protection includes protection against a particular sea chantey.

Despite his piratey-ness, Alouicious kept his word. H
made sure that the swamp and its critters were protecte
Every generation of Beaucoups was forced to read th
bloody deal and swear their fealty to it. After all, the bi
guy had spared their ancestor's life, and they were grateful.

They were merciful Beaucoups.

Of course, that was long ago, and Sonny Boy was no
Alouicious. He had no truck with flying pirates and
mythological giant furry men. So far as he was concerned,
a deal that was struck three hundred years ago was null
and void; he didn't care whose blood was on the lines, even
though he carried a few small drops of it in his own veins.

The way Sonny Boy saw it, the Sugar Man Swamp was
his and his alone, and he could do what he wanted with it.
As soon as he inherited it, he started looking for developers, people who would put a business on the property and
bring in some income. But aside from Audie Brayburn, who
owned and operated the Paradise Pies Café, they were few
and far between.

Why?

Well, for one thing, we're talking about a swamp here,
not a greeny-green pasture with gently rolling hills and
frolicking lambs. We're talking about stinging pricker vines
and high-pitched clouds of mosquitoes, of thick, humid air
that settles around your neck like a shawl; we're talking

alligators and water moccasins, carnivorous pitcher plants and primeval possums with their primeval possum babies. In short, we're *not* talking about Central Park. Nosirree.

But another thing was surely because of Audie Brayburn's insistence that the ivory-billed woodpecker could still reside there. He even claimed that he had taken a photo of it back in 1949.

Whenever anyone even considered hanging a shingle in the swamp, soon enough they heard Audie's stories, and that was that. Nobody wanted to disturb the habitat of a bird that the whole world longed for, especially after Audie convinced them that the dead trees were perfect nesting spots, that the beetles the bird loved were plentiful, that all of the conditions in the Sugar Man Swamp were just right.

It made Audie Brayburn a thorn in the side of Sonny Boy Beaucoup.

Sonny Boy Beaucoup didn't give a flip about ivory-billed woodpeckers or Audie Brayburn and his crazy stories. Did Audie have the famous one-of-a-kind photo of the bird? No, he did not.

So when Audie passed away, Sonny Boy saw it as an opportunity to take a stand. That's when he agreed to let Jaeger Stitch use two thousand acres of the Sugar Man Swamp for her Gator World Wrestling Arena and Theme

Park in exchange for half of the gate. Never mind what dear old Audie might think. He was gone. And as far as Sonny Boy was concerned, Audie's lease was up too. The only way he'd let the Brayburns stay there was if they came up with a boatload of cash. Maybe.

14

THE SUGAR MAN ALSO KNEW ABOUT AUDIE'S PASS-
ing. In the deepest, darkest part of the forest, he stirred in
his sleep. There were so many gone now. The passenger
pigeons. The black painters. The Carolina parakeets. The
mastodons. (You heard me, mastodons.) The pirates. Audie
Brayburn.

The Sugar Man missed them all.

15

IN 1947 A SCIENTIST NAMED EDWIN LAND INTRO-
duced a camera that could take an "instant photograph." He
called his invention a Polaroid Land Camera. Before then,
photographs required a darkroom and a lot of chemicals to
develop them.

A pack of film for the Polaroid Land Camera took eight
photos. Only eight. The camera was compact, too. Smaller
than a shoe box, it could be squeezed into a flat case and
carried over your shoulder with a strap.

A serious photographer knew that every shot was one of
a kind because there was no negative. Each Polaroid was
a unique print—it couldn't be reprinted. So, the shooter
took extremely good care of every photograph. As soon as
they took the shot, they would pull the photo out of the
back of the camera, gently tear it on the perforated lines
in order to separate it from the camera, then wait for a
full minute or two or three while the shot developed in its
paper wrapper. Those were a long few minutes. When the

waiting was over, it was like opening a Christmas present. Would it be as wonderful as you thought it would be? The photographer never knew until he or she peeled the back of the film from the photo and, holding it between thumb and forefinger, waved it until it was dry. The last step was to cover it with a gooey tube of coating material and wave it again. The photo was "fixed" forever . . . so long as it was kept high and dry.

That is why, if a photographer was smart, they'd place the photo in an air- and watertight container . . . such as a .30-caliber ammo can, which could be purchased at your local Army/Navy Surplus store. In addition to the photographs, campers could use these cans for storing things like matches and socks. They kept everything dry and safe.

Audie Brayburn loved his Polaroid Land Camera. But he lost it. Along with his .30-caliber ammo can. Along with his DeSoto. Lost them all in the Sugar Man Swamp, which, even though it was a good place to hide, was not a good place to lose something.

16

In the meantime, we can't forget our Scouts. When last we left them, J'miah was worrying at the foot of the longleaf pine tree, and his brother Bingo was perched at the very, very top of that same tree. J'miah squinted some more. But Bingo reveled in his discovery of Blinkle. In fact, he was having his own little jubilation moment, when . . .

Rumble-rumble-rumble-rumble!

The pine tree shimmied. Bingo tightened his grip.

"Bingo!" J'miah's voice rose in pitch. The worry level was now at the scared level.

Rumble-rumble-rumble-rumble.

The tree shook. Bingo held on as tight as he could, but as he did, the top branch swayed left, then right, then left again. Bingo heard a *ccrrreeeeaaakkk*, followed by another *rumble-rumble-rumble-rumble.*

Sway

Rumble.

Sway.

Rumble.

Sway.

There are any number of things that can make the earth tremble enough to shake a large tree and simultaneously create waves in the Bayou Tourterelle. An earthquake. A stampeding herd of buffalo. A major explosion from, say, an oil refinery.

But were any of those a factor in our story?

We can say definitively that they were not.

17

IT WAS A TENSE MOMENT AT THE TOP OF THE longleaf pine. In fact, just about the only thing that Bingo could think about was the terrible fate of Great-Uncle Banjo and how the same winds of that fate seemed to be blowing in his direction. Bingo had to wonder: If climbing trees was part of his genetic makeup, was falling out of them part of the deal? As if to make the point, a breeze pushed against the pine and made it sway again.

Left.

Right.

Left.

Right.

Bingo looked down at the bayou. Should he fall, its surface looked quite a bit friendlier than the ground. Then again, there was that whole alligator issue. He knew that if he fell into the water, he would likely live through the dive, but would he live through the jaws of the raccoon-eating alligators? It wasn't a happy thought. Bingo gripped the tree a little harder. He was clearly up a tree without a parachute.

"Bingo?" His brother's voice again. The tree swayed, the long leaves rattled. It was a message from the universe: Go Bingo! And with that, our masked tree hugger quit hugging, and with his face pointed south, he may have set a record for making it to the ground.

Once there, Bingo pulled on J'miah's paw, and together they hit the trail as fast as their stout little legs would carry them. As they ran . . . *Rumble-rumble-rumble.* The rumbles were everywhere.

Bingo had felt rumbles from thunderstorms before, but he had never felt rumbles like these, not rumbles that shook the trees, not rumbles that made waves on the bayou, not rumbles that skittered up his toes, into his belly and made his ears buzz.

With both hearts pounding like mad, he and his brother found the entryway and dodged into the cozy interior of the Sportsman. Home. Safe.

Rumble-rumble-rumble.

In a very tiny voice, J'miah asked, "What is that?"

Bingo swallowed hard. He did not have an answer. All he could do was hunker down as close to his brother as possible. The old car creaked and rattled. Bingo tucked his paws underneath his chin and stared into the darkness.

Finally, after what seemed like hours, the commotion stopped. Bingo climbed over the seat and perched on the bottom of the steering wheel. He stared at the dials and numbers on the dashboard, and hoped for some Intelligence to issue forth. He stared for a long time, but nothing happened. The Voice only spoke when there was thunder and lightning. Right now, it was as clear as could be.

Bingo drew in a deep breath. Soon enough dawn would arrive. It was time to sleep. But in that dark moment, he realized that he had never gone to bed without his parents right there with them. He sniffed the air of the quiet car and tried to smooth his tuft. This wasn't the way that freedom was supposed to feel. As if to drive home the point, he heard a quiet sniffle coming from J'miah. Oh no, not the sniffles again. But there they were, and all at once he missed Little Mama and Daddy-O like crazy. What would they do in this situation?

Of course, Bingo knew the answer. Little Mama would clean their ears, then tuck them into their bunks and kiss them, and Daddy-O would sing a song, *Fais dodo, fais dodo*. And soon enough they'd be sound asleep. Bingo felt his own little sniffle start to waft into his nose, but he swallowed hard and pushed it back.

Nope, he was not going to sniffle.

He was a Scout.

An Official Information Officer.

He gave a small salute toward the quiet dashboard. First thing in the evening, he would:

- open his eyes
- put his ear to the ground
- lift his nose to the air

He and J'miah would figure out where those rumbles were coming from and who or what was making them.

"J'miah," he whispered, not sure that his brother was awake. He continued, "Tomorrow night we have a new mission."

"We do?" J'miah's voice was a little trembly.

"Operation Rumble-Rumble-Rumble."

There was no reply.

Bingo didn't need an answer. He was filled with resolve. Then as he stretched out in his bunk, another thought popped into his head. Only this one wasn't a worry. It was a memory of looking out at the wide, starry sky from the top of the pine, a memory of the blinking red star that he, all by his little self, had discovered.

Blinkle.

Another yawn crept over him. Stars are for wishing, he thought. As soon as he woke up, he would climb another tree and make a wish on Blinkle. He wasn't sure exactly what he would wish for, but this time he'd talk J'miah into climbing with him, so that *he* could make a wish too. All at once, Bingo couldn't wait to show Blinkle to J'miah. . . . And somewhere in all this thinking about wishing and stars and his father's songs . . . he fell into a deep, deep sleep.

18

CHAPARRAL BRAYBURN DIDN'T KNOW ANYTHING AT all about Daddy-O's nighttime songs to the raccoon brothers. But he did know about the canebrake lullaby, the one his grandpa Audie had taught him.

"Whatever you do," Grandpa Audie told Chap, "don't ever try to cut the cane without singing that song."

We're not talking about any old sugarcane. We're talking about muscovado sugar, sweeter than honey, sweeter than maple syrup, sweeter than candied apples. As soon as Chap's hand was large enough to grip the machete, his mom taught him how to cut the cane, just like Grandpa Audie had taught her. It was hard, sweaty work, but it was important work too. At first, Chap had felt clumsy as he hacked his way through the thick stalks, but his mother was a good teacher. She showed him how to swing and chop, swing and chop, until he felt the rhythm of it roll up from the blade of the machete to the muscles in his neck.

After a couple of years, he was fast enough at it that his

mother turned the task over to him. "You've earned it," she said. Chap stood taller than ever, proud to be the family's "chief chopper."

"Just don't forget the lullaby," said Grandpa Audie.

Back in the day, the cane grew so thick, it made a canebrake in the bayou. That in turn made for a perfect home for rattlesnakes, *Crotalus horridus*. Canebrake rattlers. They could hide in the canebrake and wait for an unsuspecting lizard or mouse or frog to hop by, and *snip-snap-zip-zap*! No more lizard or mouse or frog.

One day, back in Aught One, when the world was still new, the Sugar Man strode his way up the banks of the bayou and reached over to grab some of that delicious cane. *Zap!* A rattler struck out and bit him on the hand. *Ouch!* And before the Sugar Man knew what was happening, *snip-snap-zip-zap* those rattlers were chomping down.

"*Ooooowwwwwwwwiiiieeeeee!*" he yelled. And with his enormous hands, he started flinging rattlers left and right. That didn't stop the rattlers. They just kept on keeping on until soon there was a whole lot of thrashing and splashing going on in the middle of the Bayou Tourterelle.

Anyone else, and he'd be dead from all that munching and crunching. But the Sugar Man was so big, and his heart was so large, that it took more than a few bites to bring him down.

But look out below! Thanks to the commotion, the alligators, which were hovering just underneath the water's surface, floated up to see what was going on. There, in the middle of the bayou, were some very succulent prey, namely canebrake rattlers.

Spicy canebrake rattlers.

It seems there was one huge alligator who started licking his chops and also slobbering a little. But it was that alligator in particular who made a fatal mistake. Well, his stomach made a fatal mistake.

It started growling . . . *gggrrrrrgggggggllllllgggglllllggrrrrrrgggglll.*

It was enough to make the snakes stop right there. They looked again, and there wasn't just one slobbering alligator; there was a whole flotilla.

Now the Sugar Man, he was a keen observer of nature, and he observed that the canebrake rattlers were about to become alligator stew. And even though he was a little annoyed at the snakes for all their *snip-snap-zip-zapping,* he didn't think they deserved to be served up al dente. Besides, he admired the way they guarded his sugarcane, even if they were a little testy.

So, he just snatched that big slobbery alligator up in his palmetto-size hands, twirled him over his head, and flung him into the air. That gator flew all the way to Oklahoma.

Well, you can imagine that none of the other gators were interested in being tossed through the sky, so they slunk underwater and floated right on down the bayou, a raft of gators, right past that wild sugarcane.

(Have we mentioned that whenever the Sugar Man got angry, he threw things? Pirates . . . snakes . . . alligators . . .)

To the snakes, it seemed like the big guy had saved their bacon, and then they felt a little bad for all that chewing they had done. In fact, they decided to let him help himself to their sugarcane any old time . . . at least for the any old time being.

Of course, the Sugar Man knew that a snake's word wasn't necessarily good to the last drop, so after that, whenever he wanted a meal of sugarcane, he sang a canebrake lullaby, a sibilant tune that put those snakes right to sleep.

> *Rock-a-by, oh canebrake rattlers*
> *Sleepy bayou, rock-a-by oh*
> *Canebrake rattlers*
> *Sssslleeeepp*

And while the snakes snoozed away, he grabbed as much cane as he wanted without all that *snip-snap-zip-zap*. Of course, he didn't take too much, only what he could eat, and a little to stash away in case he wanted a midnight snack. In the meantime, the snakes were still pretty darned happy about those gators that floated away. And even though rattlers are not predictable, they will for certain take the Sugar Man's side in an argument.

One big rattlesnake in particular, Gertrude, took a real fondness to him and decided to become his personal assistant. Yep, she hardly ever leaves his side. So if you want to do business with the Sugar Man, well, you have to deal with Gertrude first.

Of course, alligators are cagey. And last time we counted, there were plenty of them hiding in the Bayou Tourterelle.

19

THE INCIDENT BETWEEN THE SUGAR MAN AND THE rattlers happened years and years ago, back when it was just the Sugar Man and a host of critters in the swamp. Decades later, he had his encounter with the pirates. But that was long ago too. Three hundred years back. Then there was the failed posse with their ropes and axes and shotguns. That too was a century's passing.

In fact, it's been such a very long time since anyone's spotted him, or reported a sighting of him, that Sonny Boy Beaucoup made a big, fat claim: "I declare the Sugar Man officially extinct."

It was a claim that suited Sonny Boy Beaucoup. To him, the deal that his ancestor Alouicious had struck with the Sugar Man was no deal if both of the parties were no longer extant. (*Extant*. What a great word that is.)

Of course, Sonny Boy Beaucoup didn't know about Audie Brayburn's encounter with the Sugar Man. The only person

Audie had ever told was his grandson, Chap. And Chap knew better than to say anything.

Honeybees. Hornets. Honeybees. Hornets.

Moreover, nobody told the Sugar Man that he wasn't extant. How could they? He stayed holed away in the deepest, darkest part of the swamp, where news was slow to arrive. To exacerbate the situation, he let it be known that he should not be disturbed except for emergencies. For those, he placed his trust in the Official Sugar Man Swamp Scouts.

20

SPEAKING OF OUR SCOUTS, IN THE FRONT SEAT OF
the old DeSoto, Bingo rolled over onto his back. Even
though he wasn't fully awake, he rubbed his belly.

Empty, he thought.

The night before had been extremely eventful. There
had been the farewell of Little Mama and Daddy-O. There
had been the bolt of lightning and the Voice of Intelligence. There had been Mission Longleaf. There had been
rumble-rumble-rumble-rumble.

But there had not been any sustenance.

As if J'miah's stomach were in agreement with Bingo's, it
let out a loud growl from the backseat bunk. Bingo, in his
state of half sleep, wondered if he should make a quick dash
out for some dewberries before the sun rose. J'miah simultaneously wondered the same thing.

They both cracked open their eyes, they both rubbed
their bellies, they both noticed that the dark was growing

thinner, they both reminded themselves that they were, in fact, nocturnal and morning was upon them.

They both went right back to sleep.

And there you have it, sports fans: two hungry raccoons, with hours to go before they ate.

The Next Morning

21

THE SUN WAS NOT QUITE READY TO RISE WHEN Chap walked into the early morning kitchen. Once he had finally fallen asleep, he slept hard. Now he rubbed his eyes and yawned. His mom stood at the counter, mixing up the first batch of pie batter. Her hands were coated in flour. She greeted him by dabbing a thumbprint of flour onto his nose. It was an action she had done many times. Instead of giving hugs, his mother gave dabs, usually on his nose. She had done it so many times he didn't even notice it.

Instead, he stuck his finger in the batter.

"Hands out!" his mom said.

Too late. Chap scooped out a dollop of the thick, sugary mixture and stuffed it into his mouth. No matter how many times he'd eaten the sugar pie batter, it always tasted new to him, especially first thing in the morning.

"Just for that, you're going to have to pour me a cup of coffee," Mom said. His mom was a prodigious coffee drinker. His grandpa had been too.

"Coffee hounds," they called each other.

Chap reached for his mother's special mug, the one that his father had given her before Chap was born, the one that had a big pair of ruby red lips on it, faded now so that the ruby red was more like pale pink. When he grabbed it, his hand bumped against his grandpa's special mug, the one from the Twitcher's Catalogue. Chap and his mom had given it to him for Christmas a few years back. The catalog had several mugs to choose from, but they had picked the one with the great blue heron, one of Audie's favorite birds. The one on the mug spread its beautiful wide wings from the top of the rim to the base. The feathers that trailed from its head were curved in a perfect arc. "GBH," Audie had said. Great blue heron. Audie had loved that mug.

Chap thought about the GBH in Audie's sketchbook. Instead of wings wide open, the bird in Audie's book stood on the banks of the bayou. It held a large fish in its beak. Underneath, Audie had written, "You should have seen the one that got away." Chap never knew if Audie was talking about the fish or the bird. It was a mystery.

"Lots of mysteries in the swamp, old Chap," his grandpa always said.

Chap lifted the cup by its handle. There were signs of Audie everywhere. Chap felt the cloud of lonesome brush against his hair.

The huge coffee urn was full of dark, rich Community

Coffee, roasted in Baton Rouge. And even though there wasn't a drop of coffee *in* the pies, Grandpa Audie always said, "The chicory in the coffee makes the pies taste better." He followed that with, "Besides, it puts hair on your chest."

Right then Chap pulled the neck of his T-shirt out and looked down at his chest. Not a single hair. Didn't he need a few chest hairs to be a man? With that, he filled Audie's mug, right up to the brim.

"You might want to put some cream and sugar in that," his mom said.

Grandpa Audie had never used cream and sugar, had he? "Blacker 'n dirt." That's the way he had always drunk it. That was the way Chap would drink it too. He raised his grandpa's mug to his lips and took a tiny sip. It was *hot hot hot*. It was *bitter bitter bitter*. All at once, he understood how the coffee would make the pies taste better.

The sweet of the pies would offset the hot and bitter.

He set the mug down on the counter and headed for the batter again, only to be waylaid by his mom's wooden spoon. She held it between the bowl and Chap's hand.

"Out!" she exclaimed. Then she looked at the clock and told him, "Time to open." Even though his taste buds desperately needed a pie to erase the hot and bitter, he knew the upraised spoon was his cue. He walked out of the kitchen to the front door and flipped the CLOSED sign over to OPEN.

Operating hours were only from five a.m. till one p.m.—
"fishermen's hours."

Paradise Pies Café was known for its delicious fried sugar
pies, made from canebrake sugar. Audie had run the place
for more than sixty years. Back in 1949 he had signed a lease
with the Beaucoup Corporation way back when Sonny Boy
was just a tot.

While the Brayburns didn't have many customers, they
had enough.

Some of the customers, Chap knew, came as much to hear
Audie's stories as they came for the pies and coffee. And
Audie was always happy to oblige. Chap ran his tongue over
his teeth. He could still taste the bitter brew. He hoped
there were other ways to grow hair on his chest.

As he unlocked the front door, he saw a pair of enormous
headlights swing into the parking lot. He could tell that the
vehicle was definitely larger than even the duelies that some
of the local fishermen drove. In fact, it looked more like a
train than a car, a train with a single car, a train that ran on
a road instead of tracks. He'd never seen anything like it.

But as it pulled closer, he blinked. It was a Hummer. A
stretch Hummer. A *superstretch* Hummer. It looked like it could
be in two counties at once, judging by the length of it. From
Chap's spot behind the window, he saw that it took up every
single space in the parking lot and still hung out into the road.

If anyone else wanted to drive up, they'd have to park and walk. Who would drive something like that? Chap wondered. His question was answered as soon as the passengers walked through the front door. Even though there were only two of them, the pair—a man and a woman—took the largest table in the café, like they owned it or something. Right away, Chap could feel his nonexistent chest hairs rise up, along with the hair on the back of his neck. Chap knew exactly who the man was.

Unlike most of the folks who frequented the café—mostly fishermen and bird-watchers—all of whom wore overalls and T-shirts and wading boots, the man was all decked out in a fancy blue and white seersucker suit with a red bow tie. He wore white wing tip shoes, too, with the thinnest socks Chap had ever seen. The socks were so thin, Chap could see the light-colored hairs of the man's legs through the sheer knit. How would they ever protect his ankles from the biting fleas that lived in the swamp?

Chap thought the outfit was possibly the silliest getup he'd ever seen, especially for this part of the world. And even though the man was surely a grown-up, with his pale yellow-gray hair and his freckled face, he looked more like a big kid who was trying to look like a grown-up. He tapped his well-manicured fingertips on the tabletop.

The woman was a different story. She wasn't silly-looking at all. She was shorter than her companion by a head, which was saying something, because the man wasn't all that tall. Chap figured the guy might be five feet five, and that was being generous, which meant that the woman wasn't even five feet. Chap, at only twelve years, was already more than six feet tall, a trait that he had inherited from his grandpa.

"Us Brayburns are like trees," his grandpa had told him. "Tall."

The woman wore a red sleeveless tank top, the same red shade as the man's bow tie. The top accentuated her impressive biceps. Chap could tell by her arms alone, not to mention the muscles in her short, thick neck, that she could throw down the dude without any effort at all. Furthermore, she looked ready to strike without notice, rather like one of the rattlers in the canebrake. For one brief shining moment, Chap wondered if she might doze off if he sang his grandfather's lullaby.

"Pies for two," said the man. His voice snapped Chap out of his reverie. "Y-y-yessir," Chap stammered. Then he turned and hurried to the kitchen to give his mom the order. When he told her who was sitting in the café, he saw the corner of her mouth begin to twitch. When his mother was upset or unhappy, the right corner of her mouth twitched. Without a word, she handed him the coffeepot and a pair of mugs. He could feel the heat in his throat begin to rise. *Man up,* he told himself.

While Chap set the mugs on the table and filled them, he noticed that the couple had used the wide tabletop to spread out several large sheets of paper. He could tell they were plans for something. Something big. Something huge. Something that would take up at least two thousand acres.

And that's when the man said, "You must be Audie Brayburn's grandson. I'm Sonny Boy Beaucoup. And this lovely lady is Jaeger Stitch."

Chap's jaw must have dropped open six inches. As it turns out, he knew exactly who Jaeger Stitch was: the World Champion Gator Wrestler of the Northern Hemisphere. He had seen her before on television. What he didn't know was what she was doing at Paradise Pies Café at the crack of dawn.

Was she here to help Sonny Boy collect his boatload of cash? Chap's hand started to shake. Surely their lease wasn't up yet, was it? Didn't they have a little more time? He gripped the handle of the coffeepot so hard that his knuckles turned white. Hot bitter coffee sloshed inside the pot.

He knew it wouldn't be very mannish to pour the hot liquid right in Sonny Boy's lap, but he had a hard time resisting, especially when Sonny Boy looked directly at him and said, "Boy, you've got flour on your nose."

22

EVEN THOUGH HE HAD ONLY BEEN ASLEEP FOR A FEW hours, Bingo opened his eyes. It was still dark, but the air had that "in between" feel to it, that it's-not-quite-night but it's also not-quite-day-either quality.

His stomach growled. Despite his weariness from Mission Longleaf, he was having a hard time sleeping over the ruminations of his belly. What if he had a little pre-sunrise snack? What if he just slipped out of the DeSoto and grabbed a handful of ripe dewberries? What if he went right there and hurried back, lickety-split?

He knew exactly where those dewberries grew. Right around the bend near Possum Hollow. And, if he hurried, he might be able to snatch them off the vines before the possums even knew about it.

The truth was, the possums of Possum Hollow were greedy about those dewberries. And they had very sharp, pointy teeth, which they weren't afraid to use. But who made them kings of the patch?

So, *hi ho*, young Scout. It's Mission Dewberry or bust.

23

BUST? DID SOMEONE SAY BUST? CHAP WIPED THE flour off his nose. If he'd only had an egg in his hand, he would have busted it right on Sonny Boy's head.

Before he could bust something else, namely the coffeepot in his hand, his mother walked up. Chap stood beside her and rocked back and forth on his heels. His mom reached over and put her hand on his shoulder to make him stop. Together they stared at the plans spread out on the table before them.

There, in bold letters, they saw the words: "The Gator World Wrestling Arena and Theme Park."

They also saw that it would take up a significant portion of the Sugar Man Swamp. *Grandpa Audie's swamp!* While Chap stared at the plans, he realized that there would be acres and acres of concrete. How many trees would have to be chopped down? A thousand? Ten thousand? More?

The familiar flame rose up in Chap's throat. He could

see his grandfather's outstretched arms, hear his voice say, *This is paradise, old Chap.* But Chap knew that without the trees there wouldn't be much paradise. He stared at the plans, at the blank white space where the concrete would be poured for a parking lot. Suddenly, the blank white space reminded Chap of the blank white page in Grandpa Audie's sketchbook, the one left open for the ivory-billed woodpecker. If Sonny Boy's plans became real, the page would always be just that: blank. Trees didn't grow in concrete. Without the trees, the woodpecker could never come back. IBWO. Ghost bird.

Right then, Chap felt the ghost of his grandfather beside him. He rocked forward onto his toes, as if he might launch his body straight through the ceiling of the café.

Chap watched the right corner of his mother's mouth twitch again. She wiped her hands on her apron. He kept his own mouth clamped tight. Sonny Boy drawled, his voice as thick as honey, "Like I said in my notice, come up with a boatload of cash, and you can stay till the gators come home." Then he and Jaeger Stitch started laughing, like that was the most hilarious thing they'd ever heard of.

Chap gripped the handle of the coffeepot. His mother pressed down hard on his shoulder. Say something, he told himself. A man would say something, wouldn't he? So, in as calm a manner as he could muster, he said, in his lowest voice, "But what about the woodpecker?"

That sent Sonny Boy into a paroxysm of laughter. Chap waited, his jaw tightened. His mother kept her hand tight on his shoulder. Finally, Sonny Boy looked at them and tried to collect himself. But in between his guffaws he laid his right palm on the rolled-out paper and added, "That old bird is just like the raven—nevermore."

Nevermore? *Never more?* Chap couldn't stand it. Without thinking, he blurted out, "Okay. Then, what about the Sugar Man?" Immediately, he knew he had made a mistake. Even though his grandpa had never told him to keep the Sugar Man a secret, Chap understood that it was best not to bring him up. Regret raced across his face.

But instead of pressing Chap for further information, Sonny Boy and Jaeger thought *that* was the funniest thing of all.

"Look, kid," said Sonny Boy, wiping the spit off his mouth and pausing to finish his coffee. Chap waited. Then Sonny Boy delivered his lowest blow yet. "Aren't you getting a little old for fairy tales?"

In an instant, Chap's regret turned back to anger. The fire in his throat grew. He sealed his lips. Otherwise he was sure flames would shoot out. Besides, he didn't have one other thing to say. Zero. Nada. Zilch.

Sonny Boy ignored him, then smiled at Chap's mother

and told her again, "If you want to stay here, I'll need a boatload of cash."

Then together, Sonny Boy and Jaeger Stitch gathered up their plans, stood up, and pushed their chairs away from the table. They didn't do the courteous thing and push them back. They didn't even wait to eat the pies they had ordered; nor did they offer to pay for them. No, they just walked away. But before Sonny Boy went through the front door, he turned around and said, "Hey, kid. I'll make you a deal. If I see some proof of the Sugar Man, I'll give you the whole darned swamp." Then he burst into laughter again. "Yep," he said. "Nothing less." And as a parting shot, he added, "I'll sign it in blood."

Chap watched the door slam. His chest rose and fell. For a full five seconds he stood paralyzed, until at last he rushed onto the porch and watched Sonny Boy and Jaeger climb into their superstretch Hummer. As they backed out, leaving a wide pair of ruts in the red dirt of the parking lot, Chap shouted, "It's a deal!"

What he knew: He and his mom had about as much chance of filling a boat with money *or* finding proof of the Sugar Man as pigs had of flying.

24

IT'S TRUE THAT PIGS CAN'T FLY, BUT WE'RE HERE TO talk about hogs. In 1539 or thereabouts, the conquistador Hernando de Soto (after whom our Information Headquarters is named) sailed from Spain to the New World. In his company of seven ships and two caravels, there were 520 horses and 200 hogs.

You heard me. Two hundred hunky honkin' hogs!

Some of those hogs died at sea. Some of them were gobbled up by the conquistadors. But some, once the boats docked, escaped and formed their own colonies. Those were the first hogs to set foot on American soil.

It turns out that Hernando de Soto was not a very nice person. He pillaged and looted and generally wreaked mayhem wherever he went. He also wore a heavy suit of metal armor, which, unlike natural fabrics, did not "breathe." And since he didn't bathe very often, it's fair to say that he was rank. Seriously, swamp gas couldn't compete. He's buried somewhere at the bottom of the Mississippi River, and good riddance.

It also turns out that the descendants of de Soto's hogs weren't very nice either. They are still conquering parts of North America, which we'll discover soon enough.

25

I'M THINKING IT'S SOON ENOUGH, YOUNG GRASS-hoppers, because the sorry truth is, the Farrow Gang was on the march.

There are hogs, and then there are *bad* hogs (emphasis on "*bad*").

Clarification: Wild feral hogs are not to be confused with the native peccaries, also known as javelinas. Peccaries have been here all along. Just check the fossil records.

They are smaller than the hogs, and even though they look like pigs, peccaries are really not true pigs. There are some who think that they're related to the hippopotamus. Seriously. Now, don't laugh. And just like the hippopotamus, you can't round them up and turn them into pets. That's for sure.

Of course, you can't round up a wild hog and turn it into a pet either. A wild hog is just that: wild.

On the morning he was born, Buzzie's mama bellowed in glee at her son's badness. "This one is going down in boar history," she exclaimed.

Right away she named him Buzz Saw Farrow. Buzzie for short. Buzzie lived up to his name. Before he even lost his baby tusks, no boar was better at uprooting a pasture. No hog ever did so much damage to a creek bottom. He muddied it up so much that the water came to a complete standstill.

Not since those conquistador hogs stepped off Hernando's boats and cleverly escaped into the Floridian wilderness had there been such a wily hog. Not only that, but Buzzie was enormous, weighing in at almost four hundred pounds. He was a veritable buzz saw of a hog. Nothing could stop him. Nothing.

Except Clydine.

At the moment *she* was born, her daddy declared, "This is the baddest little sow I've ever seen." And she was. As soon as she could stand on her stout little legs, she tore through an entire soybean field. She ruined a season's crop of peanuts. And she plowed under a pasture where a flock full of little lambs stood cornered in the far side with nothing at all to eat. It was a sorry sight.

Clydine grew and grew and grew. Soon, she was almost as large as Buzzie. So when they met, it was a match made in hog heaven. He immediately fell in love with her soft sow's ears. She immediately went gaga over his yellow gleaming eyes and his razor-sharp tusks. He was so crazy about her that on their first date he dug up three acres of tobacco and let her chew up every leaf.

The next time they got together, she took him to a watering hole and tramped it down until there was not one drop of water left, only muck. They wallowed in it for hours.

"Buzzie," she gruntled. "You're the baddest hog I've ever met."

"Clydine," he snortled. "You're my little junkyard hog." And with that they joined forces and tore down a grove of small magnolia saplings that were just getting their new leaves, and gobbled them all up.

Soon they had a whole litter of little boars and sows. Fifteen of them. Imagine it! Seventeen bad hogs. Bad hungry hogs. Bad ravenous hogs. On the rampage. On the move. The baddest gang of wild hogs in history: The Farrow Gang.

Mothers and fathers, lock your doors. Pull the covers up to your chinny chin chins. Turn out the lights.

And here's the really bad news. One night, a terrorized fox whom they had cornered in a peanut field told them, under extreme duress, that the best, the very best, food in the entire world was the wild sugarcane that grew along the banks of the Bayou Tourterelle, the slow-moving stream that ran through the Sugar Man Swamp.

Buzzie's yellow eyes gleamed in the darkness. He charged

at the poor fox, and sent her howling through the night. Then he turned to Clydine and said, "Anything for you, my dearie dear."

And with that, they turned south, all seventeen of them, while visions of sugarcane danced in their heads.

26

AFTER JAEGER AND SONNY BOY DROVE OFF, CHAP felt an urge to throw all of the pots and pans against the wall, and he might have if it hadn't been for Sweetums.

The tall ginger cat wove his way around his boy's ankles, which had a surprisingly calming effect. While Chap gathered his wits, the cat stretched his full length, then sauntered over to his food bowl in the corner and started to munch. It was some sort of crunchy mix especially designed for "adult cats with hair balls." It wasn't the same tasty flavor as, say, fresh catfish, but altogether it wasn't that bad. And it did seem to assuage the hair balls, which, Sweetums had to admit, weren't all that attractive.

Then he remembered that he needed to let Chap know that something wasn't right with the world. Last night had brought some odd *rumble-rumble-rumble-rumble*s up through the floorboards, and he could tell they weren't the usual rumblings of the thunderstorm.

"People," he announced, "I've come bearing news."
He said it in his clearest Catalian, but to his chagrin,
they both ignored him. He meowed again. "Heads up,
people!" But instead of offering him a listening ear, Chap
told him, "You know you have to go to the back during
café hours." Of course Sweetums knew that. Duh!

The back was where the family actually lived. The front
was the café. There was a back porch, which was screened
in. And a front porch, which wasn't screened in.

Sometimes a customer chose to eat his or her pies on
the front porch, an action that Sweetums understood
because he longed, longed, longed to go out there. *Alas.*
"You're an indoor cat," Chap told him. "If you got out,
you'd eat all the baby birds."

"Baby birds would be nice," replied Sweetums, licking his
chops. But *alas* again. It was against the rules. Who made
these rules, anyways? he wondered. Were any of them written in Catalian?

He was especially not allowed into the café during business hours. Chap told him it had something to do with the
county health department and cleanliness regulations, which
was a puzzle because, "People! Can't you see that I clean my
fur all the time?" He was reasonably sure that he was cleaner
than any number of the patrons who ate their fried pies.

Then again, there was that whole hair ball thing. Humans. They had such weak stomachs. Still, hair balls notwithstanding, he knew that something was not right in the swamp. He meowed again, to no avail. For the third time that morning: *Alas!*

27

JUST A FEW MILES UP THE ROAD FROM PARADISE PIES Café, Coyoteman Jim wrapped up his overnight show on the local radio station KSUG. He stretched and yawned. The night had been long, and he was tired. The storm that had blown by had been a humdinger, and watching it on the radar had worn him out. Plus, he was worried about the Jaeger Stitch situation. He had learned about it the day before, when Jaeger and Sonny Boy came by the station to talk about airing some radio ads.

Coyoteman Jim wasn't a serious bona fide "twitcher" (a nickname for a birder), but he just loved to paddle through the dark ins and outs of the Bayou Tourterelle, looking and listening for the beautiful birds that made their homes in the Sugar Man Swamp. Like his old friend Audie, he too dreamed of one day seeing an actual ivory-billed woodpecker.

"Ghost bird," he called it. Some people named it a Lord God bird, or a good-God bird. Some called it a Lazarus bird. Others just called it IBWO, which was its official banding and spotting ID.

But to Coyoteman Jim, it was a ghost. Just like the Sugar Man himself. Something that had been there before, and still seemed to be there, even though there was no hard and fast evidence. He also knew that the bird would never, not in a million years, ever be more than a ghost if Jaeger Stitch's plans came to pass.

What would happen to the ivory-bill then? What would happen to the coots and terns and mud hens? Worse, what would happen to the Brayburns, Audie's daughter and grandson? Where would they go? The plans for the arena would surely put them out of business, especially since they called for paving over the canebrake sugar. He knew that the pies depended upon that sugar.

He took a sip of cold coffee and then set the cup on the console. Someone from the day shift would wander in pretty soon. It was time for him to sign off, so he did. "This is Coyoteman Jim, telling all you swamp critters to have a good day and a good idea." Then he held his head back and bayed, "Arrrrooooo!"

The Voice of the Sugar Man Swamp wouldn't be back on the air until that night. In the meantime, he was ready for a mug of milk and a fried sugar pie.

28

SOMEONE ELSE WAS HUNGRY TOO. OPERATION Dewberry was in full swing. In less than five minutes, Bingo made it to Possum Hollow. In the dawn's early light, he opened his eyes as wide as he could. He didn't see anything or anyone. Only a big batch of gleaming berries.

Let it be said that, in general, possums are relatively benign. But the possums in the Sugar Man Swamp are from an ancient, primeval tribe of possums, and "benign" is not how we would describe them. "Scrappy" might be a better choice of words. And they're also protective of their dewberry patch. Their *delicious* dewberry patch.

Bingo held his ear to the ground. All was quiet. There were no rumbles to be heard. He held his nose in the air. Possum scent was everywhere. But so was dewberry scent. He reached out and—"Ouch!" He had forgotten about the stinging pricker vines that the dewberries grew on. He tried again.

"Ouch, ouch, ouch." He shook his paw. Maybe this

wasn't such a great idea after all. Maybe he should go right back to the DeSoto and call it a day. Maybe . . . His belly growled. The fresh scent of dewberries filled the air.

Soon, even though he had a few stings from the pricker vines, his belly was full of ripe, juicy dewberries. He rubbed it with both of his paws. What a nice, round, tight little belly.

Buuurrrppp! Oops. He certainly hadn't meant to do that, even though he had to confess, it felt good.

So he did it again, *Buuurrrppp!* He rolled over onto his back in the cool morning air. He was in dewberry heaven. Then he felt decidedly bad that J'miah wasn't here with him, enjoying the bounty. Wasn't one of the Scout orders to be true and faithful to each other?

No problem, he thought. He would pick a pawful and take them back to the DeSoto. And just in time too, because as soon as he picked the last one—

"Step away from the dewberry patch." The voice that delivered that statement did not sound at all friendly, nor did it smell friendly or look friendly. Indeed, possums are not friendly, and this one was not playing dead.

Bingo froze. But did he drop his dewberries? The ones he had picked for his dearly beloved brother, who was at that very moment sound asleep in the old DeSoto? No, he did not. But did he scoot out of there as fast as his little legs could carry him? He did, buckaroos, he did. Yeehaw!

29

CHAP PUSHED HIS HAIR BEHIND HIS EARS. HE NEEDED a haircut. In fact, it seemed like he always needed a haircut. Every few days, his mother trimmed his bushy hair with the kitchen scissors. "It's just like the vines in the swamp," she said. "Grows just as fast."

With the exception of chest hairs, Chap was a fast grower, period. Already his shoes were two sizes larger than his grandpa's.

He remembered Audie telling him, "Son, big feet come in handy in the swamp. They're like boats and will keep you from sinking in the mud."

Boats! They needed a whole boatload of cash. Where in the world, wondered Chap, would they come up with that much money? He gritted his teeth again.

To change the subject, he reached up and turned on the small radio that sat on the sill above the café sink, just in time to hear Coyoteman Jim sign off, ". . . have a good day and a good idea."

And as the DJ's final *Arrrooooo!* filled the morning air, Chap had just that, a good idea. Hearing Coyoteman Jim's voice made him think that at least they had one reliable customer. But what they needed to increase their coffers was *more* reliable customers. And what they needed to get more customers was a good commercial on the radio. Maybe, just maybe, Coyoteman Jim would help them out.

And for the first time since Grandpa Audie had gone to meet his Maker, Chaparral Brayburn cracked a smile. If he could come up with one good idea, maybe, just maybe, he could come up with some others. He took another tiny sip of the now cold, bitter coffee. He peeked under this shirt. Chest hairs *had* to be growing.

30

Clydine and Buzzie were smiling too. Just thinking about that wild sugarcane made them downright delirious. Buzzie's yellow tusks glowed. Clydine's yellow eyes gleamed.

"Sugar," whispered Buzzie to Clydine.

"Sugar," she said to her beloved boar.

"Sugar," they said to each other.

Every wild hog in the continental USA came from stock that was imported from Europe, beginning with de Soto's Spanish sailing hogs. Most hog specialists think that they were likely Russian boars.

Spanish. Russian. Who cares?

What they were now was *wild*.

Wilder than oats. Wilder than march hares. Wilder than the west wind.

And ravenous. Did we say ravenous? Those hogs were ravenous.

31

BACK IN 1949, THERE WERE NO FERAL HOGS IN THE Sugar Man Swamp. Not one. But Audie Brayburn hadn't gone to the swamp to look for hogs.

From the time he was fifteen until he turned twenty, he worked for a bakery in southeast Houston. For those five years he worked as many hours as he could, until by 1949 he saved enough money to buy a brand-new DeSoto Sportsman.

It had always been his dream to find the ivory-billed woodpecker, ever since he was a small boy and his father gave him his first birder's journal. In fact, his nickname was Audubon, for the famous avian artist, John James Audubon. It was quickly shortened to Audie. So, once he had that DeSoto, and a little pocket change left over, he headed east, to the first place he thought he might find the elusive woodpecker—the Sugar Man Swamp.

All he took with him were his old binoculars, his sketchbook, a Hohner Marine Band harmonica and his

Polaroid Land Camera, given to him by his parents as a parting gift. He also took a .30-caliber steel ammo can, which he bought at the Army/Navy Surplus. It was airtight and watertight, perfect for keeping his matches dry, and also for storing any photos that he took on his camera. One-of-a-kind photos.

After hours of driving, he finally found his way to the Sugar Man Swamp. He had never seen so many old trees, including dead trees that were still standing, perfect trees for woodpecker nests. He parked the DeSoto, set up his camp, and settled in.

At first, the critters of the forest dodged out of his way and stayed hidden from his sight. After all, most of the humans who entered their domain brought arrows and guns and traps with them. But as the days passed, the animals began to notice that Audie wasn't toting anything except for a pair of binoculars, a camera, an ammo can, and a book that he was always scratching in. And they loved the tunes he played on his harmonica. Just loved them.

Pretty soon Audie Brayburn was considered an Honorary Swamp Critter.

One day he got out his Polaroid Land Camera, pointed it toward an armadillo, and took his shot. As soon as he pulled the back of the film from the photo, he smiled. There, printed on the slick paper, was a perfect, instant picture of a nine-banded armadillo, a surprised-looking armadillo, at that. Audie rolled a tube of gooey "coater" over the photo and waved it in the air until it was dry.

Just as he tucked the photo of the armadillo into his ammo can, he heard the unmistakable sound he had been waiting for. A sharp *kint kint* followed by *kaPOW kaPOW.*

Only one creature on the entire planet made that sound, only one. He grabbed his binoculars and his camera and followed it. His heart raced in the same rhythm—*kaPow kaPow kaPow.* He hurried, stepping as lightly as he could. He paused here and there to cock his ears. Hours passed, and the sound pulled him deeper and deeper into the woods.

As he walked, he was so intent upon keeping the beautiful bird within earshot that he failed to notice that the air had grown increasingly still. Not a single leaf fluttered. Not a single animal stirred.

Nothing except the *kint kint* of the woodpecker, and the echoing *kaPOW* of his own beating heart.

Audie Brayburn should have paid attention to all that quiet, all that stillness. If he had, he would have realized that the only time the forest became that still was right before a major storm.

Instead, he kept following the certain sound of the ivory-billed woodpecker. The air was unbearably hot, sweat soaked his clothes, the water from the swampy floor oozed into his boots, making them feel like lead weights on his feet. He was hungry and thirsty, but more than that, he was determined.

And then, just before the sun gave up for the day, Audie felt a *whoosh* of powerful wings fly just over his head, and he knew, he *knew* what it was, and with utter joy he spoke the words he'd been longing to say his whole life long. "Lord God, what a bird!"

The beautiful black wings with their trailing white feathers and the large red crest on the bird's head left no doubt. Everything about the bird said *ivory-bill*.

Audie raised his Polaroid Land Camera and snapped his shot. When he pulled the strip of film out and peeled the back off, there it was, in black and white: the broad black wings with their trailing feathers, the stripes on the sides of its neck, and the tall crest on its head. Audie opened the tube of coater and covered the surface of the shot, making sure there weren't any streaks. Then he waved the photo in the air until it dried, and slipped it into the ammo can. All just in time, because in the very next instant the rain began to fall, and there he was, deep, deep in the heart of the Sugar Man Swamp, without any idea where he was or where he had left his DeSoto Sportsman.

And worse, the rain was now erasing his footsteps. Audie

Brayburn was thoroughly and completely lost. But he was also thoroughly and completely happy. He had his photo of the ivory-billed woodpecker. But just in case he got the chance to take another shot, he checked the camera, and because it was getting so dark, he popped one of the small flashbulbs into the socket. He'd prove to the world that the bird was not extinct—that is, if he could ever find his way back to his car.

For a moment, he stood there, soaking wet, first from sweat and then from the big drops of rain that slid out of the sky. He had no idea which direction to go. He also noticed a dry scratch in the back of his throat.

Not only that, but it was getting darker and darker. There is hardly any place on earth that is darker than a swamp at night, especially in a rainstorm. All Audie knew was that somewhere he had left his brand-new 1949 DeSoto Sportsman, and if he could only find his way to the car, then he could take shelter.

He squeezed his camera shut, slung it across his shoulders, and hoped that the rain wouldn't ruin it. He wished he could store it in the ammo can, but it was too large for that. At least, he thought, the prized photos would stay dry. He patted the can and hugged it to his chest.

For hours he pushed his way through the swamp, tripping over tree roots and sloshing through shallow pools of muck. He was soaked through and through, covered in mud. He kept patting his ammo can, to reassure himself that the photos inside it were safe and dry. He knew that no one would take him seriously if he claimed to have seen the ivory-billed woodpecker without proof. The photograph was his proof.

"Suitable for framing," Audie announced. Yep. And even though he was thoroughly lost, he felt enormously lucky. And happy, too. So happy. And, he noticed, his nose was becoming increasingly stuffed up.

He finally reached a clearing and held his head back, mouth open in the pouring rain, to try to quench his thirst. He rubbed his neck while he gulped at the drops. But despite the heavy downpour, it didn't seem as though he could take in enough to slake his thirst. He lapped at it with his tongue and stood there for a long time, face toward the sky, eyes closed. The scratch began to burn.

Finally, when he thought he might drown from facing into the rain, luck found him once more. He opened his eyes and looked ahead just as a bolt of lightning slashed through the rain-soaked trees. And there, he was sure of it, in that momentary flash, sat the DeSoto.

Oh, sweet salvation!

He stumbled toward the automobile, which had been waiting there all those long hours. Just as he approached it, another bolt of lightning cracked so close that it lifted Audie right out of his waterlogged boots.

It lit up the whole area, so that he could clearly see the car now, with its beautiful mud-caked grille. Not only that, but the hood ornament, the bust of the conquistador, glowed in the dark. The bolt of lightning must have activated the battery, he thought. In that moment, Audie Brayburn had never loved anything so much as he loved that car.

He stumbled into the backseat and began to shiver. His throat felt raw, as if he had swallowed pricker vines. All he wanted to do was curl up in the dryness of the DeSoto and go to sleep.

The seats of a 1949 DeSoto are made of soft leather, with straight, solid stitches. They're wide and roomy, too. Perfect for a weary explorer to lie down and sleep. The last thing that Audie Brayburn did before he drifted off was open up his Polaroid Land Camera so that it could dry out. He was still holding it on his stomach when at last he closed his eyes.

Soon, it felt like the car was rocking, rocking, rocking.

Sometime in the middle of the night, he felt a *bump*, and when he did, he accidentally hit the button on the Polaroid, which still sat on his stomach. He woke just as the flashbulb popped. For a second he was blinded by the reflection of the flash against the car's window.

Instinctively, he pulled the film out of the back of the camera. He likely would not have seen the photo if another bolt of lightning hadn't struck nearby. But it did, and there, in the brief flash, he saw a fuzzy face framed by the windows of the car. Audie blinked. He thought of all the fuzzy faces in the woods—raccoons, possums, bears. Now he had a photo of one, but in the darkness he couldn't tell exactly what it was. On top of that, the fever coursing through his body made everything blurry. He sat up for a moment, the photo in his hand. He peeled the backing off and set it on the floorboard. Then he covered the photo with coater, blew on it, and slipped it into the ammo can with the others.

The camera only held eight shots. Now there were only five more left on that roll, and it reminded him that sooner rather than later, he'd run out of supplies and have to leave the swamp and head home.

But before then, he had to sleep. He was so, so, so sleepy. So very sleepy . . .

32

AFTER HIS NARROW ESCAPE FROM THE PRIMEVAL possum, Bingo slipped into the DeSoto, carrying his pawful of dewberries for his brother. But when he looked over the seat back, he noticed that J'miah was sawing logs. Hmm . . . Now he was faced with a conundrum. Should he wake J'miah up with the good news about the dewberries? He had, after all, risked being attacked by a primeval possum.

Then again, he *had* risked being attacked by a primeval possum. Maybe, Bingo thought, I deserve these dewberries.

But wasn't one of the Scout orders "Be true to each other"?

Would it be untrue to eat the dewberries if he had picked them for J'miah? Of course, it might also be untrue to wake J'miah. What if he was having a wonderful dream or something, and didn't *want* to be disturbed? Bingo had to admit that J'miah looked very cozy.

Decisions, decisions.

The sweet scent of dewberries filled the air of Information Headquarters. Then there were the dewberries themselves to consider. Would it be untrue to the dewberries if he let them go uneaten? What was true and what was not?

Alas! All of these questions made Bingo feel a little dizzy. He sniffed the dewberries. From the backseat he heard J'miah roll over. He waited one moment longer to see if his brother was going to stir. If J'miah woke up by himself, the dewberries were his.

Wait.

Wait.

Waaaiiittt.

There was nothing left to do but gobble those delicious dewberries down. Which he did. In one huge bite.

Buuuuurp!

Oh, dear. Bingo had not meant to do that. He covered his mouth with his paw. Maybe J'miah had not heard it.

Too late.

In Bingo's ears, he heard his brother say, "Mmm . . . dewberries."

Thankfully, the next thing he heard was *Zzzzzzzz.*

33

MEANWHILE, IN THE DEEPEST, DARKEST PART OF THE forest, Gertrude uncoiled her very lengthy body and rattled her tail, *chichichichichi*. She felt itchy. Fleas! Who knew that a snake could be bothered by fleas? Then again, Gertrude wasn't your run-of-the-mill ordinary snake. She was the Sugar Man's familiar. *Crotalus horridus GIGAN-TICUS.*

CHG!

Gertrude blinked until her eyes finally adjusted to the darkness, and when they did, she noticed that her old companion was snoozing away, as usual. Even with all his fur, the fleas did not seem to bother him.

She gave him a little nudge, but he barely budged, just snored a little louder. Satisfied that he was sleeping soundly, Gertrude slithered out of the dark lair and slipped into the muddy bayou. Ahh, the cool water felt good on her scaly skin.

Once in a while a girl just needs a bath. She swam to

and fro for several minutes, gobbled up a couple of tasty bullfrogs, and then slid back to her nest.

She sighed. "That's better." She curled up into a huge coil and slid back into sleep.

Chichichichichi.

34

SOMEONE ELSE WAS FEELING ITCHY: JAEGER STITCH. In fact, she was itching for a fight. She flexed the muscles in her biceps and clenched her fists. Raw power surged through her compact body. With Sunny Boy Beaucoup sitting on the backseat of the Hummer beside her, her first impulse was to put him in a headlock and make him beg for mercy.

But she fought down the urge to do that. After all, he was her primary source of funding for the Gator World Wrestling Arena and Theme Park.

Her fingers twitched. She needed a fresh alligator. With the early morning sun beginning to peek through the branches of the cypress trees, she could see the swamp from the passenger window.

A few miles down the road from Paradise Pies Café—after their driver, a college student named Leroy who was trying to pick up a few bucks during summer break, had set the Hummer on cruise control—she demanded, "Leroy! Stop the car!"

Leroy hit the brakes, which made the heavy vehicle slide down the gravel road. It dug deep trenches with all four of its enormous steel-belted radials. A cloud of red dust surrounded them. Before Sonny Boy could even say, "What the . . ." Jaeger jumped out the door and disappeared into the trees, leaving Sonny Boy in the backseat of the Hummer.

Sonny Boy straightened his red bow tie and admired his thin, elegant socks. For all of two seconds he considered following her. But that would mean ruining yet another pair of socks. He decided to wait in the car. If Jaeger wanted to tramp around in the swamp and wrestle an alligator, far be it from him to stop her. He had no real affection for the lady wrestler. She was a business partner, nothing else. He and the driver . . . What was his name? Larry? Lonny? James? Whatever. He and the driver would wait.

He knew that Jaeger would find an alligator toot sweet, and from there it would just be a matter of minutes before she had it belly up and snoring. (Fact: When alligators are flipped onto their backs, they fall asleep. Jaeger was a pro at flipping them.)

In the meantime, Sonny Boy could use the quiet time

without Jaeger to dream about the boatloads of cash that the Gator World Wrestling Arena and Theme Park were going to deliver to him. If he thought at all about "*the wrath of the Sugar Man,*" those words that were written in his great-great-greater-greatest-grandfather's own blood, it was only fleetingly. In fact, he was so absorbed by his visions of all that moolah, he didn't notice the *rumble-rumble-rumble-rumble*s that came up through the floorboards and shook the big car.

He didn't notice. But Leroy did. They made him chew on his fingernails.

35

BACK IN THE CANEBRAKE, THE RATTLESNAKES WERE abuzz. They had also noticed the *rumble-rumble-rumble-rumble*s, and it made them edgy.

Snip-snap-zip-zap. Snip-snap-zip-zap. Snip-snap-zip-zap.

36

WHILE SONNY BOY SAT IN THE BACKSEAT OF THE
Hummer, and Leroy chewed on his fingernails, Jaeger
Stitch stepped quietly onto the soft wet floor of the swamp.
The sun rose through the tree branches just enough to
light the path in front of her. She was only feet away from
an unusually deep bend in the Bayou Tourterelle when
she smelled the gators.

At this early hour they'd be calm, thanks to the cool air
that still lingered from the night. Nevertheless, her senses
were heightened. A calm alligator is still an alligator, and
she knew that.

Sure enough, there, right along the bank, was her prey,
a six-footer. Not the biggest gator she had ever wrestled,
but not the smallest, either. It was just right for a fight.

Before the gator could even flip on its go switch, Jaeger
Stitch landed on its back. *Ooomph!* She pulled its jaw up
into a ninety-degree angle and kissed the tip of its nose. As
if that weren't humiliating enough to the poor gator, she

grabbed its toothy snout and pulled it over onto its back and started rubbing its belly. In fewer than five minutes, the alligator was in dream city.

And Jaeger Stitch was back in the superstretch Hummer. She ran her fingers through Sonny Boy's yellow-gray hair. He covered his nose with his silk hanky to circumvent her reptilian smell. She took a deep breath. Nothing like the odor of alligator at sunrise, she thought. Then she closed her eyes, leaned against the seat back of the enormous car, and hummed to herself as they rolled through the morning mist.

The Next Night

37

TEXAS IS HOME TO THOUSANDS OF ALLIGATORS. It's impossible to put a definite figure on their population. Let's just say that every waterway between the Sabine River to the east and the Pecos to the west has its share of the toothy beasts. And once in a while one is found in a lake or stream west of that.

The same could basically be said about the porkers, although their range is definitely bigger and wider than that of the gators. Biologists estimate that the number of feral hogs in the USA range from between two and four million animals in thirty-nine states. More than a million of them can be found in Texas alone, giving Texas a big, fat porcine problem.

Hogs like to hide out along creek beds, where they lay low in the underbrush so that no one can see their sneaky selves. Like our raccoons, they're also nocturnal, using the cover of darkness to mask their dastardly deeds.

They usually travel in family groups called sounders. Isn't that a great word? "Sounders"? We just love that.

But do we love Buzzie and Clydine and the Farrow Gang? Friends, there is nothing to love there.

Nothing.

38

Bingo was done with sleeping. All day he had tossed and turned. Between the wonder of discovering Blinkle, the worry of the mysterious rumbles, his close encounter with the primeval possum, and his wee bit of guilt over not sharing the dewberries with J'miah, it had been a long day. Staying asleep had been a struggle. So, he was glad to see the dark of evening begin to rise.

Then, like an alarm clock, his belly growled and he realized he was hungry again. He gave himself a big shake and stretched. He knew that he and J'miah had a mission to accomplish, Operation Rumble-Rumble-Rumble. They had to figure out what was making all that racket. But even a mission can't stand between a raccoon and a meal.

In the backseat J'miah stretched too. "I'm starving."

Considering his own new state of starvation, Bingo blithely erased his guilty feelings about the dewberries . . . sort of. Then he announced, "Crawdad Lane." Crawdads would be just the thing. A power breakfast to get them through Operation Rumble-Rumble-Rumble.

"Bingo!" said J'miah. (Bingo hated it when J'miah did that, but we think it's kind of funny.)

Crawdad Lane wasn't very far away, right along the edge of a narrow bend near the bayou.

"Let's go," said Bingo.

"Crawdads over easy," added J'miah.

They scooted out the entryway. At the opening, they both opened their eyes, put their noses in the air, and put their ears to the ground. No rumbles. None.

In no time at all, our Scouts were busy digging up craw-dads. It wasn't long till the two of them were lying on their backs in the cool mud along the water's edge, their bellies stuffed like water balloons.

From his spot in the mud, Bingo looked up through the tree branches. He could see the clouds gathering. He took a deep breath. Rain. Rain was surely on the way. But as he watched the clouds tumble by, he could see an occasional star twinkle above the trees. Each one looked as though it might be hanging in the boughs, a little like a sparkly firefly. He craned his neck to see if he could spot the red one. Just the memory of it made him happy.

Alas, he thought, too many clouds.

He might have stayed there for the rest of the night,

except . . . *rumble-rumble-rumble-rumble*. There it was. Only now, it seemed to be even closer. Bingo sat up. Thanks to his stuffed belly, he groaned a little.

"What *is* that?" he asked.

Then there was a repeat. *Rumble-rumble-rumble-rumble.*

"What—"

Rumble-rumble-rumble-rumble. Bingo grabbed his stuffed belly and felt just a wee bit queasy.

Rumble-rumble-rumble-rumble.

As if that weren't enough, *split splat splitter splatter.* The clouds that Bingo had just watched bunched up and let loose. And then . . . *Zap!* A thin, jagged line of lightning slipped from the sky.

Bingo and J'miah looked at each other knowingly. Without missing a beat, they ran back to Information Headquarters, scurried through the opening, and shook their coats.

Outside, *ZAPP!* . . . another bolt of lightning sliced through the sky. Bingo could see sparks dance all around the perimeter of the car. He was glad he was indoors. He stared through the vine-covered windshield and could just see the light on the hood ornament through the leaves. The bust of Hernando glowed. It was a weird orange color, and from where Bingo sat, he could only see the back of the conquistador's head.

Bingo looked at the dials on the dash, and sure enough, their purplish lights began to flicker on and off, until they finally illuminated the numbers that went from one to twelve in a circle, and just like always . . . *oooooowwwweeeeeee* . . . *blip* . . . *blip* . . . *weeeeooo* . . . *ssshhhshshshshshsh* . . . followed by the Voice of Intelligence, loud and clear.

"Howdy there, east Texas. Hope everyone is in a nice, dry spot while these storms pass through."

Bingo cocked his ears. So did J'miah. Then *blip* . . . *blip* . . . *blip* . . . *blip*. The Voice came back on, "Fishing should be good down on the bayou. . . ." That made Bingo happy. He loved fish. He'd go fishing first thing.

"Fishing," said J'miah.

The radio kept going . . . *ooooowwwwweeeee* . . . *weeeeeoooo* . . . and then they heard words like . . . "terrible" . . . "horrible" . . . "no good" . . . "very bad" . . . *wwweeeeoooo* . . .

Bingo's tuft stood straight up.

"What?" asked Bingo.

"Who?" asked J'miah.

They both waited.

Sure enough the worst words of all, ". . . HOGS! . . . they're heading directly toward the Sugar Man Swamp. . . ."

Bingo and J'miah looked at each other. "The Farrow Gang!" they said together.

Then . . . *blip* . . . *blip* . . . *ooooweeeee* . . . The purple lights dimmed and the message faded, but right before it ended, there was a *crackle* . . . *pop* . . . *pop* . . . "Arrroooo!"

Raccoon fur went *poof, poof!*

Bingo and J'miah looked like stripy puffer fishes. They had never heard the Voice howl before. But the howl was not nearly so unsettling as the news that the notorious Farrow Gang was heading their way.

Buzzie and Clydine's reputation had preceded them. Our Scouts, with their open eyes, sniffing noses, and ears to the ground, had seen first-paw the devastation wrought by the Farrows. Over the past several months, lots of critters had sought refuge in the Sugar Man Swamp to avoid being mowed down by the hogs. Bingo had seen the white-tail deer hobble in, their legs battered and bruised. He had witnessed a cattle egret with its wing torn and tattered. He remembered the small flock of cottontail rabbits, their paws sore from running too many miles in their efforts to get away from the gang.

They were the lucky ones, the ones who made it to the welcoming domain of the swamp. Until now it was believed that the swamp meant safety, but . . . *rumble-rumble-rumble-rumble* . . . Bingo swallowed hard. If the Voice of Intelligence told the truth (and it always had), the Sugar Man Swamp, and all the critters who dwelt there, would soon be under siege.

All at once, our Scouts knew what they had to do. They didn't particularly want to do it. They'd never done it before. But it had to be done.

Together, Bingo said to J'miah and J'miah said to Bingo, "We have to wake up the Sugar Man."

39

IN A SMALL BUILDING THAT SAT DIRECTLY UNDER-
neath Bingo's blinking red star, Coyoteman Jim watched the
rain pouring outside his studio window. Of course, like most
radio stations, it was soundproof, but he could still see the
flashes of lightning in the distance. He looked at the clock
on his desk. Midnight. He pushed away from the micro-
phone, took the headphones off, stood up, and stretched.

He had just finished the weather report and the unsettling news about hogs, and had lined up a long set of his
favorite songs. He only halfway listened to them as they
spun from one to another in the automatic player.

He was looking for some inspiration. The previous morning, when he had stopped in for his fried sugar pie and mug
of milk, Chap Brayburn had asked him to make a commercial for Paradise Pies. But right now he was stumped. There
was a blank pad of paper and a pencil on the desk in front
of him, but all it had on it were some doodles and scribbles,
nothing else.

He knew how important this advertisement would be. If the Brayburns could get some more customers, and make some extra cash, they might be able to slow down the plans being hatched by Jaeger Stitch and Sonny Boy Beaucoup. It was a long shot at best. He knew that. He also knew he needed to make a humdinger of a commercial if they were going to convince customers to drive all the way down the Beaten Track to eat sugar pies.

Coyoteman Jim rubbed his eyes. The station felt lonely, what with the rain and all. This was usually about the time when his old friend Audie would have called him, just to say hello, and maybe to tell him a story.

Audie wasn't his only caller. Because Coyoteman Jim worked the graveyard shift, people tended to call in after everyone else had gone to bed. It was downright surprising what folks felt like they could tell him in the wee hours of the morning. Some things were worth repeating, like when Sissy Morton won the baton twirling competition in Baton Rouge; and when the Whites had their new baby girl, Emma Kathleen; and the time that Brother Hadley at the Little Church on the Bayou got bit by a copperhead and lived to tell about it. Those things were happy news, and Coyoteman Jim was totally down with sharing them.

But there were a lot of things that weren't necessarily meant for the public at large, like when Billy Willy Curtis called to tell him that his big sister Mae Rae Curtis sat under the tanning lights for so long, she turned completely orange; or when Cousin Ida called to say that her mother Aunt Erla had dropped the Thanksgiving turkey on the floor but didn't let on, so everyone ate dirty turkey and didn't know it; and the time when Maynard Douglas called to say his youth pastor at the Little Church on the Bayou drank so much Mountain Dew, it snorted out of his nose when he laughed.

These were items that Coyoteman Jim kept to himself.

Which is the reason that he ended every graveyard shift with a major howl. Instead of saying all those things that shouldn't be said, he just cut loose with a big ol' *Aaarrroooooo!*

So there wasn't much happening in the KSUG listening area that Coyoteman Jim wasn't aware of, even though there were a few things he wished he didn't know. Like the invasion of the hogs, for example. *Yet another introduced species*, thought Coyoteman Jim. And that included those other introduced species: Sonny Boy and Jaeger.

As he slipped his headphones back on over his ears, the strains of the last song zipped into his head. *Shake, shake, shake* . . . Wait! He turned up the volume. *Shake, shake, shake* . . . Yes! There it was—the inspiration for his commercial. *Shake, shake, shake* . . . It was perfect. He listened to the tune one more time, put his pencil to paper, and started writing.

40

BINGO AND J'MIAH WERE WORRIED. FROM THE SAFETY of Information Headquarters, they could feel the *rumble-rumble-rumble-rumble* as the invasion approached. They knew they needed to wake up the Sugar Man to tell him that the swamp was under attack. And they also knew that they didn't have much time. These things they knew.

What they didn't know was how they were going to go about waking up the Sugar Man without getting *snip-snap-zip-zapped* by Gertrude.

And as if all of that wasn't enough to worry about, they weren't even sure where to find the Sugar Man. No one had actually seen him in years, maybe decades. Not even the famous Great-Uncle Banjo had claimed to have an encounter with the Sugar Man.

It wasn't like there was a sign on the door somewhere: "Here Lives the Sugar Man." It wasn't as if there was a neon arrow pointing to his secret lair: "Sugar Man's Hideaway."

It wasn't as though there was a map with a big, fat circle around "Sugar Man Villa." Nope.

All they knew was that they would have to head toward the deepest, darkest part of the swamp, where the trees blocked out all the light, where the underbrush was so thick that even noises couldn't penetrate the thick vines and leaves.

"Brrr . . ." Bingo shivered just thinking about it. He looked out at the driving rain. J'miah shivered too.

And even though it goes against the grain for raccoons to move about in daylight, they decided to wait for the morning, when hopefully the rain would stop and they could use the sun's rays to help them find the Sugar Man's deep, dark lair.

To keep himself busy, J'miah decided to resume Mission Clean-Up Headquarters. Raccoons in general are similar to pack rats. They collect all kinds of odd items, and over the years, the backseat had become something of a pit. It bothered J'miah. He liked for things to be tidy and neat. Especially when he was nervous. Like now.

All at once, Mission Clean-Up Headquarters turned into a disinfecting frenzy. First, J'miah wiped down the insides of all the windows with some fresh leaves. He rubbed and rubbed until each window was sparkly. Of course, he couldn't see through them because the outside was pretty much covered with vines, but at least he could see the vines better.

Next, he used a small branch as a broom to sweep off the old leather seats. It was surprising how much clutter had accumulated back there over the years.

Bingo did his best to stay out of his brother's way. He decided to do some chin-ups from the rearview mirror so as not to get swept up with the debris. J'miah ignored him and kept sweeping. Soon he had a whole collection of rubbish piled up on the floorboard behind the passenger's side. It was like a small landfill between the seats.

Bingo clung to the rearview mirror. He decided then to reverse himself and hang upside down. It gave him a different perspective on the inside of the DeSoto, not to mention a unique view of his brother. Watching J'miah in all of his industriousness made Bingo wonder if he shouldn't feel just a tad bit guilty for hanging out and not joining J'miah in the cleanup? Then again . . . nah . . . That wonder fleeted.

J'miah continued to sweep, pausing every now and then to adjust his invisible thinking cap. It was during one of these cap adjustment breaks that he decided that he simply couldn't live with that landfill of rubbish. So he made a declaration. "We're going to shove this stuff through the entryway."

"Huh?" said Bingo, still hanging upside down.

"Yep," replied J'miah. The plan was to cram the garbage underneath the seat so that it could then be shoved through the door. The instructions were perfectly clear.

So he set his broom down and began to shove . . . and shove . . . and shove. But the landfill did not move.

Bingo continued to do his bat impersonation.

J'miah shoved some more. The pile of rubbish shifted, but it did not move.

"There must be a blockage," said J'miah. And seeing that Bingo was no help, J'miah climbed over the seat and crawled down to the floorboard and peered underneath. Sure enough, there was something large and square. He reached for it with his nimble paws. It was cool and smooth to the touch. He grabbed it by the corner and tugged, but it wouldn't move. Whatever the large square thing was, it was wedged tight.

J'miah pulled on it again, but there was no getting it to move. He shoved his head under the seat to get a closer look. First he examined the front of it. He noticed that there was a handle. He grabbed hold of it, but no matter how hard he pulled, the blockage stayed put. Then he moved to the right side of it. Nothing.

By now Bingo was feeling the effects of being upside down, so he let go and dropped to the floorboard and peeked underneath the seat. Sure enough, he saw the blockage too. "Why haven't we ever noticed this before?" he asked.

J'miah said, "Because we never swept out the garbage before!" Did we detect a note of testiness coming out of J'miah? Why yes, we believe we did. But Bingo decided to ignore it.

Still, the blockage was a mystery. He was just about to crawl under there too when he heard a distinct *pop!* Bingo's tuft stood straight up. "What was that?" he asked.

J'miah had discovered a wire spring on the side of the box, and when he pulled it forward, for the first time in more than sixty years, it popped open with a rush of sixty-plus-year-old air. But because the hinges were a little rusted, our raccoon could only get the lid to open a tiny crack, only wide enough to stick his curious little paw deep inside it.

At first, he couldn't feel anything. Nothing. Just the cool, smooth interior of the metal box. So he reached a little farther.

Nothing.

Farther.

Noth— Something!

Sure enough, he felt something.

A leaf? It felt like a leaf. Only not exactly a leaf. It was thicker than a leaf. Stiffer than a leaf.

He gave it a tug. Out it came, a piece of square white

paper, but it wasn't like the paper that he had found wrapped around soup cans, or the rough paper that turned into mush when it got wet. This was a different kind of paper. It was slick and shiny. J'miah lifted it to his nose and sniffed. It had an odd smell, not like the grass or the flowers or even the bayou. Rather it was something pungent and a little sticky. Then he turned the papery object over and discovered that the other side wasn't white at all. Instead, it was gray with a darker gray and black shape on it.

An armadillo! J'miah brushed his discovery off on his fur, and the image grew shiny.

"Art!" he exclaimed. The square papery thingie was art! He crept out from under the seat and held it in front of Bingo's face. "Look!"

"Hmm . . . ," Bingo said. He looked at it closely. The image was clearly an armadillo. He had never seen an actual rendering of an armadillo before, and frankly, he had never found armadillos to be all that attractive. They were in the possum category, so far as he was concerned, and they had very squinty eyes and rather ratlike tails.

Nevertheless, there was an armadillo in two dimensions. Yes, he thought, it must be art. Then he watched J'miah gently place it right on the front dashboard so that both of them could admire it.

J'miah sat back and studied it. Every home should have

some art, that's what he had always believed, and just because he and Bingo lived in Information Headquarters did not mean that they couldn't have some art. He squinted his eyes and focused on the armadillo. It was way better than the occasional bottle cap or gum wrapper that he had found on the banks of the bayou.

He loved it even though it was just an ordinary armadillo. And the more he studied it, the more he thought that the armadillo looked a little surprised, as if the artist had caught it off guard.

While the rain poured all around them, the raccoon brothers stood side by side and admired their new decoration. It was a happy moment in Scoutville.

41

LET'S RECALL ANOTHER EVENING OF DRIVING RAIN, when someone else waited in the DeSoto. Yep, Audie Brayburn. Can you remember how he had just taken that photo of the Lord God bird? How he had stumbled, exhausted, into the swamp and finally found his way back to his car? How he fell, into the backseat, into a deep, deep sleep? How he felt a bump in the night?

Can you recall all that? It was way back in 1949, more than sixty years ago. Well, while he slept, there were three things that Audie Brayburn, Honorary Swamp Critter, didn't know.

A. There was so much rain that night that the water came out of the banks of the Bayou Tourterelle. It pushed its way across the bottomlands of the swamp and eventually poured underneath the 1949 DeSoto Sportsman and began to carry it away. The big whitewall tires let the car float, sending it directly toward the overflowing bayou, which was rolling faster than ever.

Audie was in a boat that was doomed to sink. The DeSoto weighed a ton and a half, and even with four large floaty tires, the weight would take it to the bottom soon enough.

B. Audie Brayburn wasn't only tired from lack of food and water. He was burning up with fever. He had a serious case of swamp flu. We're talking dire straits, sisters and brothers. The rocking of the car by the water did not wake him up. It only made him sleepier.

C. The Sugar Man Swamp Scouts were on the job. Over the previous days, Bingo and J'miah's great-great-greater-greatest-grandparents had kept an eye on the young man as he'd wandered through their forest, and they could see that he seemed to love the place as much as they did. Plus, they absolutely adored those tunes he played on his Hohner Marine Band Harmonica. They did not want him to end up at the bottom of the Bayou Tourterelle.

For now we'll leave the rest of Audie's escape from certain death to your imagination. What we know is that the DeSoto came to rest on a small knoll along a high bank that overlooked the bayou, and after a day or two, Audie woke up and tried to turn the car on, but the engine was so soaked with water, it refused to start. So Audie, still spacey from his flu, stuffed his ammo can with its one-of-a-kind photos underneath the passenger seat, stumbled out of the car, and weakly tramped his way to the highway, where a passing motorist spied him and rushed him to the hospital in Port Arthur.

Later, much later, after he recovered from the flu, even though Audie looked and looked and looked, for the rest of his life he looked, he never could find that Lord God bird or the old DeSoto again.

42

CHICHICHICHICHI. GERTRUDE SHOOK HER LONG RATTLY tail. Despite the cool relief of the rain, she felt itchy again. Those fleas were driving her crazy. She decided she needed to scratch. But how does a rattlesnake scratch? She doesn't have any hands or fingers or paws, after all. Nope. So she wrapped herself around and around and around a big cypress tree, and rubbed and rubbed and rubbed. She rubbed so hard that she came right out of that itchy skin.

"Ahh," she said. "That's better."

She scanned her beautiful new golden skin, with its dazzling black diamonds. She wished her snoozy companion would wake up and help her admire it. She gave him a nudge with her nose.

Nothing.

She gave him another nudge.

Again, nothing.

She knew she could probably wake him up with a little

snip-snap-zip-zap, but that would make him cranky. Who needed that? She could cook up a batch of cranky all by her lonesome. Nope, *snip-snap-zip-zap* wasn't the answer.

She looked at her beautiful new skin again. The diamonds were gleaming in the darkness of the lair. It seemed a waste that there was no one to show it to.

She shook her tail as loud as she could. *CHICHICHI-CHICHI.*

All Mr. Sleeper did was reach over and give her a gentle pat on the head and roll over. Alas. Time for the last resort. Sugarcane. She knew that if he got one whiff of that canebrake sugar, he would wake right up. She looked in the knothole where she kept her supplies. There was not one single bit of sugarcane left.

Sugarcane, it turns out, is the only thing aside from a rattlesnake bite that will wake up the Sugar Man. She'd have to order some, she thought. But that was no great consolation, because she'd have to wait for a courier to take her order.

You might be surprised to learn about the Snapping Turtle Courier Service. Turtles? Couriers? Turtles? Couriers?

We know!

It just so happens that in the water, turtles are fairly zippy. They could swim up and down the Bayou Tourterelle in the blink of an eye. Moreover, snapping turtles weren't at all concerned about Gertrude. So she used their services from time to time, especially when she needed to restock the sugarcane.

But at that moment, Gertrude realized that she had not seen a courier in a while. Turns out they were keeping their heads down. As they should.

Rumble-rumble-rumble-rumble.

Gertrude would have to wait.

43

MEANWHILE, SEVENTEEN HOGS WERE NOT WAITING. A little rain was no deterrent. They were now within a couple of nights' hog-trot to the Sugar Man Swamp. Clydine lifted her piggy snout in the air. "I want me some wild sugarcane," she said with a snort.

"Me too." Buzzie grunted.

The fifteen younger Farrows snorted and grunted in agreement. The sounder had been marauding through the countryside all night long, and the first rays of sunlight were peering through the clouds. Like we said, hogs are nocturnal, so it was time to take a nap.

Soon enough, they found a shallow creek bottom. Of course, Buzzie and Clydine charged at the unsuspecting deer who made the grave mistake of strolling by.

Next, the terrible twosome frightened a pair of squirrels with a whole array of snorts and squeals. And let's not forget the loud hoorahs toward a pack of surprised coyotes.

Those coyotes didn't even whine. They just tucked tail and ran.

The hogs were having a big ol' laugh at all the scaredy-cats. "Ha-ha, hoo-hoo!" As the stars lay down, however, so did the hogs. But just as they settled in for their day-long snoozefest, an immense cloud of mosquitoes landed on the hogs' bristly backs and dug in.

There are only a few critters on this whole blessed planet that aren't afraid of wild hogs. Mosquitoes are one of them.

Buuuuzzzzzz! They whined and whined, and then they dined and dined.

Clydine squealed like a baby, *"Wheeeee . . . aaaahhhhhh . . . wwwwaaahhhhh!"*

Buzzie squealed too. *"Whheeeeee . . . aaaahhhhh . . . wwwwaaahhhhhh!"*

The Farrow Gang squealed and squealed and squealed.

Mosquitoes couldn't care less about all that squealing. They were enjoying their ham and bacon breakfast.

"Mud!" Buzzie squealed. "We need mud." And with that, they tore into that creek bottom. They splashed and rolled and smashed and crashed until there was no water at all, just muck, muck, muck. Whatever small drops were left turned around and ran uphill. "Losers," called the hogs. Then they wallowed and wallowed and wallowed.

Ooohhheeee, that muck felt great. The seventeen Farrows snortled and gruntled in glee. In glee, I tell you. Finally, they were coated in so much mud, the mosquitoes could not bite through it. You could say that it soothed the savage beasts.

For the time being, that is.

The Second Day

44

AT PARADISE PIES CAFÉ, THE FIRST ROUND OF CUS-
tomers had already come and gone; a couple of regular fishermen and a young guy named Steve, who showed up because
he made a wrong turn. Even though Steve only stopped by to
ask for directions, Chap talked him into ordering a sugar pie.
As soon as Steve tried it, he ordered another one.

"Dang," Steve said. "These are delicious." He smacked
his lips. It made Chap feel good. Not at all the way he felt
after Sonny Boy and Jaeger's visit the morning before.

Then Steve said, "Too bad you're so far off the beaten
track." Considering he had lived on Beaten Track Road his
whole life, Chap was used to the old joke.

"No, really," Steve said. "Y'all are hard to find." He added,
"I'm not sure I can even figure out how to get out of here,
much less come back. Even my GPS is flaky out here." To
prove it Steve held up his shiny phone with the blank screen.

So Chap drew him a map on one of the paper napkins,
and told him that the state highway wasn't that far away. It
just seemed like it because the road was so narrow. Steve

thanked him. Then he ordered one more pie to take with him, and waved good-bye.

After Steve left, the café was completely empty, and it was barely six a.m. They'd only been open an hour. Chap hoped against hope that Steve wouldn't be their last customer for the day. He went to clean off Steve's table, when he saw it: the cell phone. Oh no! Chap grabbed it and rushed out the door, but it was too late. Steve was gone.

"Oh well," said Chap. He carried the phone into the café and set it on the windowsill next to the radio. That was the official spot for lost and found. Usually the items that were lost were things like baseball caps or maybe a cigarette lighter. Things that weren't valuable. A cell phone was valuable. At least this one was.

"He'll be back," said his mom, pulling out a chair and sitting down. In her hand was her bottomless cup of coffee.

Not for the first time, Chap noticed that her lips were almost the same color as the pale pink lips on the side of her mug; the mug had been a gift from his father before he died in a motorcycle accident. Chap had never known his dad. The accident was before he was born. After it happened, his mom moved back in with Audie, and they had been there ever since. Ever since Chap's whole life. Once in a while someone would ask him if he missed his father, but how could he miss someone he had never even met?

Nevertheless, even though she never said so, Chap knew his mother missed him, especially when she said, "You look so much like your father." Then she would pat him on the cheek, or worse, dab his face with flour. He rubbed his face to make sure there wasn't a dab on there that he was unaware of. His mom could be tricky like that.

In front of her was a stack of dollar bills and a few coins. He watched as she re-counted them. Then she folded the bills in half and stuck them into her apron pocket.

"It's not a boatload," she told him, "but it's a start." To Chap, the small stack looked measly. And the café looked way too empty. They needed a yacht full of customers, he thought. As if it agreed, the coffee urn gurgled. Hearing it made him think about being a man again.

Coffee.

Chest hairs.

Coffee.

Chest hairs.

Yesterday Chap had managed to drink roughly one quarter of the cup. He decided to try again. He reached for Grandpa Audie's Twitcher's Catalog mug and filled it to the top. Once again it was *hot hot hot. Bitter bitter bitter.* To Chap, it tasted like acid going down his gullet. There had to be a less painful way to become a man, especially now when everyone told him that's what he was supposed to be.

But for the moment, staring at the empty café, he felt completely helpless. *Man up*, he told himself. He took a big gulp of Community Coffee. That was a mistake. It burned on the way down. He decided from then on he would only take sips. Tiny sips. He looked in the cup. There was still two-thirds of the blacker 'n dirt liquid left, but he couldn't bear to drink any more. Nevertheless, progress had been made. Yesterday, he drank a quarter of a cup. Today, he drank a third. Maybe tomorrow, he'd drink a half. He carried his grandpa's cup to the kitchen and set it on the counter. The GBH seemed to stare out at him, its wide wings spread as it flew in a circle around the cup.

Seeing the bird made Chap want to compare it to the one in Grandpa Audie's sketchbook, which was still stashed away under his bed. Since there was nothing for him to do in the quiet café, he walked to the back of the house, careful not to let Sweetums through the door into the café. He plopped across his bed on his stomach and pulled the book out. Sweetums curled up next to him on the bed and started to purr.

"Person, can you not see that I'm trying to sleep?" asked Sweetums.

Chap ignored the cat and opened the book.

Sweetums tucked his head under his paws.

As Chap turned the pages, his grandpa's scent wrapped itself around him. He felt the familiar heat rise up in his throat. He swallowed it down. Page by page, he gazed at his grandpa's renditions of the fauna of the swamp. Not only were there birds, but there were minks and muskrats and lizards too, every one of which Audie had seen at least once, probably more. As the years had passed, he had added pages to the book. It was heavy and thick, filled with swamp critters. There they were, in Audie's funny style, the pencil lines distinct in their thickness. There was no subtlety in Audie's drawing. It was more like cartoons than art.

Chap flipped through the pages, looking for the GBH. Where was it? He wished that the book was alphabetical, but instead it was what Audie called "incidental." As in, "Incidentally, I saw a Canadian goose today," or "Incidentally, I almost stepped on a green anole," or "Incidentally, have you seen the baby teals?" After each incident, he got out his pencil and drew the incidental subjects.

Chap turned the last page. He must have skipped over the heron—not surprising, since some of the pages tended to stick together, a result of the sugar. When you deal with sugar day in and day out, it tends to coat things, including sketchbook pages. Chap turned the pages again, this time from back to front, taking care to gently pull some of the stuck pages apart.

It was upon such a pulling that he noticed the drawing of the raccoon. Audie had featured the raccoon playing a harmonica. "Raccoons," he said, "are multi-talented." It was a funny picture. Chap had looked at it dozens of times. It was one of his favorites. He stared at it for a full minute; so long, in fact, that he could practically hear the notes of the harmonica slipping out of the drawing.

But then he remembered that it wasn't the raccoon he was looking for, it was the heron. He turned another page, only to realize that it too was stuck.

The page felt almost crisp from age and sugar. At last, he managed to pull it apart. There, staring at him, a drawing he had seen dozens of times before but had forgotten: the Sugar Man!

Chap slammed the book shut and sat up. Sweetums, startled, jumped off the bed and scurried underneath it. Chap's heart raced. Sonny Boy's words echoed in his ears. *If I see some proof of the Sugar Man, I'll give you the whole darned swamp.*

"Proof!" said Chap, right out loud.

Without apologizing to poor Sweetums, Chap grabbed the book and ran straight for the kitchen.

"Mom," he called. "Look what I found."

Chap held the familiar sugarcoated page up to her. His face beamed. But what Chap failed to see, and what his mother had to point out to him, was the date Audie had scratched at the bottom of the picture: 1949.

"Honey," she said, "even if Grandpa really did see the Sugar Man, this was drawn more than sixty years ago. Nobody else has claimed to see him since even before then."

Chap looked at the date. His face fell. He wanted to argue with his mother, but in his heart of hearts, he knew she was right. A drawing from 1949 wouldn't prove anything.

45

THE 1949 DESOTO SPORTED A "ROCKET" BODY, WITH a beautiful waterfall grille, a grille that seemed to smile.

It also had a Simplimatic transmission, making for a smooth ride. It was so smooth that in one of their advertisements, a passenger asked the driver, "New road?" To which the driver replied, "No, new DeSoto!"

46

ADVERTISEMENT? DID SOMEONE SAY ADVERTISEMENT? Coyoteman Jim worked for hours, perfecting his radio commercial for Paradise Pies. As soon as he signed off with his customary, "This is Coyoteman Jim telling you to have a good day and a good idea," followed by his signature howl, he slipped into the production room and made a recording.

He got it down on the first try. The only thing left to do was take it to Paradise Pies and let Chap and his mother give it their nods of approval. He slipped the copy of the recording into his jacket pocket and headed out the door.

Meanwhile, at the café, Chap needed to do something. Anything. The disappointment of the drawing, combined with his feelings of being outmanned by Sonny Boy and Jaeger, all on top of a small power surge from the one-third cup of coffee, made him feel like an unlit bottle rocket.

His mom, sensing his short fuse, gave him a chore. "We need some fresh cane," she said.

Yes! Chap untied his apron, hung it on a hook by the

back door, and reached for his muck boots. He turned them upside down and shook them first to be sure nothing was nesting inside them, like a brown recluse spider or a scorpion. Satisfied the boots were empty, he slid his feet into them. Then he grabbed his grandpa's old machete and headed out. The heft of the machete felt solid in his hand.

Chopping cane was not for the faint of heart, not only because the machete was sharp enough to slice off a finger or a toe, but also because of the canebrake rattlers. So the first thing to be done, of course, was the lullaby. As Chap neared the canebrake, he started to hum, and as he got closer, he lifted his voice and sang his grandpa's tune:

Rock-a-by, oh canebrake rattlers
Sleepy bayou, rock-a-by oh
Canebrake rattlers
Sssslleeeepp

Right there, underneath the boiling Texas sun, Chap stood up a little taller. Gripped the machete a little firmer. Sweated a lot more profusely. In fact, despite the fact that it was his mother who taught him how to do it, Chap realized just then that chopping cane was . . . oh, yes it was . . . wait for it . . . *manly!*

In less than an hour, he chopped out a bushel of fresh

sugar. He bundled it together with a length of twine and tied it with a knot, just like Audie had shown him. The fresh, sweet odor of sugar filled the air.

"There's nothing like it," Audie had told him. And there wasn't.

But cane wasn't the only thing that Chap knew how to chop. He had used this very same machete in his almost daily forays through the swamp with Grandpa Audie. Chap knew how to use the wide blade to clear a path through the stinging vines that covered the forest floor and crept up the trunks of the trees.

Thinking about chopping his way through the woods made Chap think of his grandpa's long search for the DeSoto.

And for possibly the millionth time in his twelve years on Earth, Chap asked, "Where is it?" For a long moment he gazed at the banks of the Bayou Tourterelle, with the stalks of cane racing to the sky, and scanned the landscape for any sign of the old car.

Nothing. It was a ghost car. Just like the ivory-billed woodpecker was a ghost bird. The cloud of lonesome bunched up above his head.

And as if the rattlesnakes sensed his keening, they started to buzz. *Chichichichi . . .*

That was Chap's signal to skedaddle. He tugged on the

sugarcane and headed back to the café. As he pulled the bundle into the kitchen, for possibly the billionth time in his twelve long years, his mother greeted him with a dab of flour, this time on his cheek.

"Mom!" he said. Was that any way to treat a man?

As Chap wiped his cheek, Coyoteman Jim walked through the front door. Seeing him, Chap's pulse quickened. Maybe, he thought, just maybe, the radio man had come up with a great commercial, one that would encourage customers from far and wide to drop in and try one of their delicious fried sugar pies, even if they had a hard time finding them along the Beaten Track Road.

And then Chap had another good idea—signs! He could make some signs. As if it agreed, the morning sun shot a beam of light against the front windowpane, and the air inside the café turned golden, like a fresh fried pie.

47

Bingo and J'miah didn't need a sign to know that there was trouble brewing. All night long there had been *rumble-rumble-rumble-rumbling*. The horrible, terrible, very bad, no good Farrow Gang was closing in.

It was time to launch Operation Rumble-Rumble-Rumble into action. With the sun filtering its way through the trees' branches, with only their wits and their whiskers, Bingo and J'miah set out to find the Sugar Man. They scampered through the entryway of the DeSoto and stepped into the warm, wet air.

They were not at all used to such brightness. It took a moment for their eyes to adjust. They also felt very exposed, out in the open as they were. They had to pause for a moment to adjust to this idea that they could actually be observed by any of the daytime creatures, creatures they only vaguely knew about.

J'miah pulled his invisible thinking cap around to shield his eyes. It wasn't very helpful, being invisible and all. They may have stood there all morning, in the unfamiliar light of day, but finally Bingo took a step forward, and that seemed to break the spell.

Tally ho, young Scouts.

And forward they went. Without any solid directions, they simply started walking. Whenever the trail reached a fork, they turned toward whichever lane seemed darkest. They walked and walked and walked, and sure enough, the forest grew thicker. It began to close in on them, blocking out the light above.

Hours passed, and the shadows grew longer and longer. As the trees and bushes became ever more dense, the forest grew quieter. Bingo strained his ears to hear crickets. Not a single chirp. J'miah listened hard for cicadas. Nary a buzz.

Dark.

Quiet.

Dark.

Quiet.

Bingo was extremely glad that he had J'miah with him. J'miah was over-the-moon happy that he was with Bingo. Suddenly in the dark and quiet, they heard, *chichichichi*.

Bingo looked at J'miah. J'miah looked at Bingo, and together they said, "Gertrude!"

And Gertrude said, "Sssscccouts! Just who I need."

48

RACCOONS ARE ONE OF THE LARGEST MEMBERS OF the Procyonidae family, a family that includes ringtails, kinkajous, olingos, coatis, and cacomistles. (Don't you just love those names?) They are such a handsome group, with their thick fur and their stripy tails; but despite their relatively long claws, and their sharp teeth, their primary form of defense is to go into emergency poof mode, which makes them look five or six times larger than they actually are. The second that Bingo and J'miah came nose to nose with the world's most itchy rattlesnake, their fur went *POOF* and *POOF*, respectively.

While they stood next to each other, trembling and poofing, Gertrude circled them with her long, sleek body and said this unexpected thing: "I've been waiting for sssssssomeone to drop by. And what do you know? Here you are."

Of course Bingo and J'miah immediately thought she had been waiting to have them for dinner, and not to *share* dinner either.

Bingo blurted out, "I don't think we'd t-t-taste very good."

But to their surprise, Gertrude started laughing. "Sssssilly Sssscout, I don't eat anything with fur. It getsss ssstuck in my throat."

That, it goes without saying, was a relief . . . but not a whole lot. Okay, some. A little. There was still a lot of poofing, not to mention shivering, still occurring between the daring duo.

Then J'miah said, "What did you need us for, then?" Bingo could feel his tuft standing straight up.

"I need ssssomeone to admire my new sssskin," Gertrude said. And with that, she pulled the brothers together even more tightly inside the circle of her body. That way they could get a very up-close-and-personal look at all of her black diamonds. The raccoon brothers were effusive in their praise.

"My, those diamonds are definitely impressive."

"I've never seen scales like these."

"You could win the Swamp Critters Beauty Pageant."

"There is no one more lovely in these whole deep, dark woods."

They went on and on.

Finally, satisfied that the raccoons had adequately admired her new skin, she asked, "Just out of curiossssity, Sssssscouts, what bringsssss you to the deepesssst, darkesssst part of the ssssswamp?"

J'miah blurted out, "Rumbles!"

"Lots of rumbles," added Bingo.

Then they told her that the Sugar Man Swamp was about to be besieged by . . .

"Horrible," said Bingo.

"Terrible," said J'miah.

"The Farrow Gang!" they said together.

"We have to wake up the Sugar Man," said J'miah.

"It's our Scout duty," said Bingo.

"He's the only one who can stop them," they chorused.

"Of coursssse," she agreed. "I could give him a little *snip-snap-zip-zap*." She paused. "However, that might make him out of sssssorts."

Bingo and J'miah both recalled their parents' warnings about the *wrath of the Sugar Man*.

Bingo gulped. "Isn't there another way?" he asked.

"Oh, yesssss," said Gertrude. "The besssst way to wake him up issss with the ssssweet aroma of fresh ssssugarcane. Only one itsssy-bitsssy problem. I regret to tell you that we're completely, totally, utterly out of sssstock."

It only took about five split seconds for Bingo and J'miah to come to the conclusion that Operation Rumble-Rumble-Rumble now had a new step in the mission: procure some fresh sugarcane to wave underneath the nose of the Sugar Man so that he would wake up without any wrath. And that meant a trip to the edge of the Bayou Tourterelle, where the canebrake grew, which was closer to the DeSoto than to the Sugar Man's hideout.

They'd have to make the long trek back with the sun on the wane. Did that deter our Scouts?

"We have to hurry," said Bingo.

"We have to scurry," said J'miah.

And without even telling Gertrude adios, they took off. They retraced their steps, turning toward the light, lighter, lightest forks in the road as they went, which was a problem because the sun was now getting lower and lower in the sky. So far, they had not heard any further rumbles, but they knew that as the nighttime drew near, the hogs would wake up and continue their steady march toward the swamp.

Bingo and J'miah ran and ran and ran. Soon their tongues were hanging out. Their legs were tired and their paws were sore. They were panting for breath, but sure enough they finally reached the canebrake.

Victory!

Eeeeerrrrrrrtttttt. Step on the brakes!

Canebrake rattlers everywhere. *Crotalus horridus!* The nastiest of the pit vipers, known for their razor-sharp fangs and their stinging venom.

Chichichichi! Suddenly Bingo and J'miah were met by a

hive of buzzing snakes, all poised to strike. If our young raccoon brothers dared try to snatch even one itsy-bitsy-teensy-weensy cane of sugar, you know what they'd get?

Snip-snap-zip-zap!

Bingo's tuft was too scared to pop up. J'miah's eyebrows were too scared to squint. It was terror time in Scoutville. All at once, they realized that no one had ever told them what to do in the face of a writhing, wriggling, hissing horde of angry pit vipers. And they were completely in the dark about the lullaby. (Lullaby? What lullaby?) For the second time in one afternoon . . . *POOOOOOFFFF!* and *POOOOOOFFFF!*

Every single strand of fur stood straight up in a brilliant display of gray and black. Did their poofability slow down the stunned *Crotalus horridus*? Only for a split second. But that, sports fans, was just long enough for our heroes to go into full-bore retreat.

49

AFTER HEARING THE ADVERTISEMENT THAT COYOTE-
man Jim had made for them, Chap and his mom were certain
that tomorrow would bring a whole bevy of new customers.
They just knew it would.

To cap it off, Jim had stayed all morning and helped Chap
turn some old boards that Chap had found in the boat shed
into signs. There were three of them, and Coyoteman Jim
promised to place them along the road:

Sign one: "Turn here for the best fried pies in the world."
Sign two: "Only two miles to fried sugar pies!"
Sign three: "You're almost there!"

They had used a spray can of Day-Glo orange paint that
Grandpa Audie had bought years ago, the purpose of which
nobody could remember. None of the signs were exactly
artistic, and the paint ran down from the letters.

"It doesn't matter," said Coyoteman Jim. "They only need

to catch the eye." They were definitely eye-catching. Chap knew that for sure.

After the café closed that afternoon, and Coyoteman Jim went on his way, Chap and his mom set to work. They pre-fried at least ten dozen sugar pies in anticipation. All they had to do in the morning was quick-fry them again, and they'd be delicious. If it didn't work, they'd have a lot of leftover pies. And fried pies weren't all that great when they were more than a day old. After that they'd have to be tossed into the bayou for the catfish.

There was so much riding on Coyoteman Jim's commercial.

As soon as they were finished in the kitchen, Chap took it upon himself to get the boat ready to fill with cash. The boat was a two-man pirogue, a sturdy, flat-bottomed affair with a pointed bow that raised up a few inches out of the water, and a square stern that helped keep it stable.

Chap pulled the old pirogue out of the boat shed, where it was stored. He tugged and pulled and tugged and pulled, up the steps and then set it smack in the middle of the screened-in back porch. The boat had always seemed rather small before, but parked in the middle of the porch, it looked huge. When he imagined having to fill it with cash, it looked enormous.

For comparison's sake, he cut a dollar-size piece of paper

from his school notebook and watched it float down down down into the boat's bottom. The paper looked very small. It was going to take a lot of bills to load that boat.

He tried not to let himself think about Sonny Boy and his deal. After all, what chance was there of finding any proof of the Sugar Man? Nevertheless, a small bead of hope nested right underneath his chin. He scratched at it, just like he might scratch at a mosquito bite. The more he scratched it, the more it stung. He stuck his hand into his pocket so that he could leave it alone.

He climbed into the boat and sat on the bench. It felt funny, sitting in the boat on the back porch. It felt even funnier when Sweetums jumped into his lap. Chap rubbed the cat from nose to tail. Sweetums purred so loud, Chap thought the cat might pop. And that's when they heard the rumbles. Sweetums dug his claws into Chap's thighs. "Person," said the cat in perfect Catalian, "do you not hear those rumbles?"

"Ouch," said Chap, lifting the cat into his arms. "It's just a thunderstorm, that's all." Chap breathed in. He could smell the oncoming rain, even though he knew it was still in the distance. "Yep," he said, "it's storm season, all right."

But Sweetums knew that wasn't all. Something else was rumbling out there. Something big and nasty. *Rumble-rumble-rumble-rumble.* See? It made him hiss, which made Chap laugh.

Hmmph! Is there anything worse to a cat than being ridiculed? We think not. Sweetums jumped out of Chap's arms and headed for the bedroom, where he dodged underneath the bed and started grooming himself.

Indeed!

Chap stood up and stretched. He needed grooming too. With all that baking, he had a fine dusting of flour coating his skin, including yet another dab on his forehead put there by his mother. It was time for a shower, and then lights-out. The morning would come way too soon.

The Third Night

50

INSIDE THE DESOTO, BINGO AND J'MIAH FINALLY stopped panting after their narrow escape from the canebrake rattlers.

"Whew," said Bingo.

J'miah had a wee case of sniffles. He didn't want to think about how close he had come to being a tasty snack for the snake community, so he steered his sights toward something happier, namely the picture of the surprised armadillo. It made him feel a little better.

But Bingo did not feel better. He wished that he had been able to wake up the Sugar Man. He wished that Gertrude had not run out of sugarcane. He wished that the rattlers weren't so snippy. He wished, wished, wished.

But all that wishing didn't change one thing. The Sugar Man was still asleep. The rattlers were still abuzz. And the rumblers still loomed. It seemed to him as though there should be something they could do to obtain some of that sugarcane without getting all *snip-snap-zip-zapped*. The entire safety of the swamp depended upon it!

He wished he knew what that something was.

And then, all at once, he did.

"Blinkle!" he exclaimed. The star. His blinking red star that he had only just discovered two nights before. Blinkle. His very own wishing star. Operation Rumble-Rumble-Rumble would have to be momentarily shelved and replaced with Operation Blinkle.

"Come on," he said to J'miah.

J'miah crossed his paws. If Bingo thought that J'miah was going to go back out there with those snipper-snappers, he was crazy.

Bingo tugged on his brother's paw.

J'miah tugged back. "Nope," he said. Then, just to make sure that Bingo had gotten the message, he said, "Nope, nope, nope. Not gonna do it. Nosirree."

"Hmmph," said Bingo. He could see that J'miah was not in a budging frame of mind. With a sigh he said, "Fine. I'll go by myself then." And he let go of his brother's paw and turned toward the exit.

J'miah squinted.

"I'm really going now," said Bingo.

J'miah put his paws over his ears.

"Good-bye," said Bingo. "I hope I see you again sometime."

J'miah tried to block out the noise, but that last sentence tore right through his stripy gray fur and smacked him, right in the belly. In his ears, he could hear Little Mama reciting the Scout Orders, especially the one that went "be true and faithful to each other." How could he let Bingo go out into the night alone? He couldn't. And, as if to seal the deal . . . *rumble-rumble-rumble-rumble.*

J'miah slapped his forehead with his paw, and once again, against his better judgment, he followed Bingo through the entryway on the passenger side in search of a tall pine tree. This time they took the long way so as to avoid *Crotalus horridus.*

As they neared the tree, Bingo's sore paws felt better. *Climb,* they seemed to say. So that's exactly what he did. He climbed. J'miah, meanwhile, stood at the base of the tree and waited. He couldn't watch. But he could keep his nose in the air and his ears to the ground. And he tried not to think about Great-Uncle Banjo, or hogs . . . or rattlesnakes.

Above him, Bingo scurried to the very top of the tree. There he twisted around from one side of a branch to another, and looked out. He could see the clouds beginning to assemble. He sniffed the air. Rain was nigh, he could tell. He twisted around again . . . and . . . there it was, his blinking red star.

"Blinkle," he whispered. Then he closed his eyes. There was a chant he was supposed to say. Something Daddy-O taught him long ago. He concentrated hard. What was it?

The star blinked on and off, on and off, on and off. He tapped his toes on the branch in time with the blinks. Soon, the rhythm of it reminded him of the chant. Yes!

"Blinkle, Blinkle, little star. How I wonder what you are . . ." But that was as far as he got. What was the rest of the chant? He wished he could borrow J'miah's thinking cap. Stars. Weren't there dozens of poems about stars? Maybe he could mix them up and make his own star chant for his own new star.

Think, Bingo, think.

Then, Bingo! "I've got it," he said. "I wish I may, I wish I might, have this wish I wish tonight."

Of course! He knew that. And he also knew exactly what to wish for: sugar. Canebrake sugar. In any form he could get it.

Suddenly, he felt a whole lot better. Maybe Operation Rumble-Rumble-Rumble wasn't over yet. He whispered to Blinkle, "Thank you." All in good time, too, because as soon as he said it, the gathering clouds bunched up and made all of the stars, including Blinkle, disappear.

Bingo scampered down the longleaf pine tree, tapped J'miah on the shoulder, and together they hurried back to the DeSoto. He had no idea how, or even *if* his wish would come true, but he definitely felt better for having made it.

Operation Blinkle: accomplished.

51

ON A DIFFERENT PORCH—IN FACT, ON THE VERANDA OF
the Beaucoups' impressive French colonial–style
Homestead—Sonny Boy and Jaeger sipped their mint
juleps and smacked their lips. Nobody actually lived at
the Homestead anymore. It was only visited on the occasional weekend and holiday. In fact, since his childhood,
Sonny Boy had only been there a few times in his adult
life, preferring his palatial mansion in Houston to the
ancient family place.

Nevertheless, it was perfect for his purposes now. He
could stay there while he oversaw the building of the Gator
World Wrestling Arena and Theme Park. That way, he
wouldn't have to put unnecessary miles on the Hummer. It
was astonishing how few miles to the gallon the thing got.
It was definitely a gas hog.

Even though rain loomed, for the moment the sun was
setting over the perfectly groomed azaleas. The recently
installed mosquito-misters were dispatching the mosquitoes

left and right. The distinct aroma of citronella wafted through the air. Sonny Boy and Jaeger weren't exactly having a party, since neither of them particularly liked each other. But they were reveling in their plans for swamp domination.

In the glow of the tiki torches, Jaeger looked at Sonny Boy over the rim of her frosty glass and thought for the umpteenth time how much she'd love to grab him in a neck lock and flip him over her back. In his ridiculous seersucker outfit, he posed such an easy target. Then again, she thought, it would be *so easy* that she doubted she'd get any satisfaction out of it. If there was one thing she loved, it was a challenge.

For his part, Sonny Boy knew that Jaeger had evil designs on him, but he also knew that he was Mr. Moneybags, the source of funding for her road-show attraction. He knew that as long as he controlled the purse strings, he was safe. And, he had to admit, he admired her pluck, not to mention her skills at taking down large reptiles.

"Jaeger, my dear," said Sonny Boy, interrupting their sunset reverie. "What would you say to a groundbreaking ceremony, to kick things off?"

This caught Jaeger off guard. She had vaguely thought about a grand opening ceremony after the park was built. But she had not considered a groundbreaking ceremony before it even opened.

Sonny Boy continued, "It would stir up excitement. Plus, we could invite all the dignitaries."

Dignitaries. Jaeger liked the sound of this. While she was at the pinnacle of the alligator-wrestling crowd—indeed, she was rather like a goddess in that bunch—none of them consisted of *dignitaries*. Dignitaries were in an entirely different social milieu. Mingling with dignitaries would definitely enhance her quest for fame and fortune. She liked it. Her urge to toss Sonny Boy . . . lessened.

"Tell me more," she said. She wanted details.

While they sipped their juleps, they began to make a list of Sonny Boy's influential friends—friends in high places, that is. When Sonny Boy wrote down the mayor and the mayor's husband, Jaeger even had an odd urge to . . . Well, okay . . . She briefly thought about kissing Sonny Boy, an urge that both disgusted her and thrilled her all at the same time. It was the same with kissing alligators. Thrill, disgust, thrill, disgust. You get the picture.

So, instead of throwing Sonny over her back, she threw her glass. It burst against the porch rail in a very satisfying chimelike crash. Shards of crystal and mint gleamed in the torchlight. She looked at her compadre with a new appreciation. The day she had met Sonny Boy Beaucoups had been a lucky one for Jaeger Stitch.

A lucky day indeed.

52

How had they met, anyways? Let's just say it had to do with a gambling casino in New Orleans, and a bad roll of the dice.

53

AFTER JAEGER BID HIM GOOD NIGHT AND RETIRED TO her room, Sonny Boy grimaced. The crystal glass had been in his family for generations. One of his great-grandmothers had bought it in Venice at the turn of the century. That was the story, at any rate. Sonny Boy knew that it was more likely that one of his buccaneering grandfathers had lifted it from a Venetian cruise vessel as it sailed into Galveston Bay.

Indeed, the old homestead was filled with artifacts, both gainfully acquired and not. A stroll through its many rooms was like a trip to the museum. There were shelves filled with crystal and silver and objets d'art. There were silk tapestries hung on the dining room walls. And there were bronze and marble sculptures in the sculpture garden.

Above the fireplace in the library there was a commanding portrait of the family founder, Alouicious Beaucoup, leering down at his descendants from his perch above the mantel. Upon close inspection, it was obvious that the frame was made of an old ship's railing. How apt.

And just beneath the portrait, resting on the mantel, was the framed deal he had supposedly struck with the Sugar Man, written in the ancient mariner's blood, the same deal that had, according to legend, saved Alouicious's life.

Sonny Boy used to revel in his ancestor's impressive gaze, but lately he found it unsettling. He couldn't escape the feeling that the eyes in the portrait were watching him. So he covered the painting up with a fine linen tablecloth. As for the bloody deal, he simply turned it over, facedown on the mantel. The deal remained on its face, but the cloth over the portrait wouldn't stay put. It kept slipping off.

Sonny Boy tried stapling it, but the wood of the frame was too hard for the staples. Then he used superglue, but that didn't hold either. Even after he fastened it with duct tape, the cloth came free and slid down onto the hearth in a heap. After that, Sonny Boy stopped going into the library and locked the door.

That didn't work either. Every time he passed by, the door hung open, and the portrait stared at him. Sonny Boy got to where whenever he had to walk past the library, he picked up his pace and ran, so as to avoid the room and the painting altogether. Instead he sought refuge in the study. Unlike the formal setting of the library, with all of those leather-bound tomes and the austere gaze of this great-great-greater-greatest-grandfather, not to mention the promise struck in blood, the study felt cozy. He also liked the glass cases that lined the walls. He particularly liked the aged brandy in the crystal decanter. "Perfect," he said.

The Beaucoups were known far and wide as collectors, and some of the things they collected were specimens. Animal and bird specimens. As a child, Sonny Boy had ignored the specimens. In fact, he had refused to look at them. The old, dead animals with their glass eyes gave him the creeps. But tonight, a glass of aged brandy in his hand, he studied them with admiration. He could tell they were as fine as those in the Smithsonian. And just as rare.

And that's when his eye fell on the bird.

"Lord God," he said, splashing his brandy on his seersucker sleeve and dripping it onto the mahogany floorboards. How had he missed it in all these years? Even he knew, by its red crown, that it was a fully grown male. Its impressive black wings, with their trailing white feathers, were spread out to their full three-foot-wide span. It seemed to soar in place. Ghost bird.

Sonny Boy threw back the rest of his brandy in one huge gulp. It burned on the way down. He leaned in to get a better look. That's when he noticed the faded handwritten note. "Collected in September 1949, by Quenton Beaucoup, in the Sugar Man Swamp."

For the second time that night, Sonny Boy grimaced. His

father, Quenton Beaucoup, had died in a freak accident in the swamp. One day, he went out hunting with his bird dogs, Sam and Pete. Several days later, the dogs returned without him. And several days after that, Quenton's body was found in the top of a tree. The autopsy said "heart attack," but no one could explain why he was so far up in the tree. "Scouting for birds," was the official line. Afterwards, his mother had packed Sonny Boy up and moved to Houston, which was fine by Sonny Boy. He preferred the big city to the remote swamp.

He didn't have much memory of his father. Sonny Boy was barely a toddler when his father had died. And besides, what he remembered of his father wasn't all that pleasant. Quenton Beaucoup seemed to like his dogs more than he liked his son. As Sonny Boy recalled, he himself liked the dogs more than he liked his father.

Sonny Boy reached for the decanter of brandy and refilled his glass. So, he thought, Audie Brayburn's tale of taking a photo of the bird in 1949 wasn't so far-fetched after all. He looked at the specimen in front of him. The infamous lost photo might even have been of this very bird.

He shook his head. It didn't matter. Just because the bird had been alive in 1949 didn't mean there were any left now, more than sixty years later.

He took another sip of brandy and let it rest on his

tongue. It tasted sour. If, by some miracle, another ivory-billed woodpecker were to show up, the plans he and Jaeger Stitch were making would be doomed. Only a few years ago, rumors of a ghost bird had been reported in Arkansas, and suddenly the area had been besieged by birders and environmentalists and scientists and reporters and tourists.

While the Sugar Man Swamp belonged to him, Sonny Boy Beaucoup, the protests of the twitchers would be so loud and strong, he'd never be allowed to build even so much as a boat shed on his land, much less a theme park.

Sonny Boy looked at the mounted bird in the back of the glass case. Its golden brown eyes glistened. As he swallowed his sour brandy, a small bundle of old-fashioned jitters rose up inside Sonny Boy Beaucoup, starting at the bottom of his thin socks until it hissed through the top of his yellow-gray head. And for the second time in one night, another crystal glass went flying through the air.

54

In their deep, dark lair, Gertrude stirred, but not enough to open her eyes. She knew all about the "official" line about Quenton, the one about "heart attack." But she also knew about the unofficial line: *"wrath of the Sugar Man."*

A deal was a deal, after all.

55

As soon as the Scouts scampered back through the entryway of the DeSoto, the rain took on a kind of fury.

"Just in time," Bingo said. Making his wish had definitely made him feel better. He raised his front paws, yawned, and stretched. He was so ready for a nice, long nap.

What Bingo didn't know was that J'miah had also made a wish. He wished that climbing didn't make him feel so much like throwing up. He didn't know how effective his wish could be, since he didn't have a personal star like his brother did. His wish hadn't made him feel better.

He crossed his paws and sulked.

What did make J'miah feel better was . . . art. J'miah loved the art he had found of the surprised armadillo. It still sat perched on the dashboard, and every time he looked at it, it made him feel happy. Happier, at any rate. As happy as he could feel in the face of the temporary suspension of Operation Rumble-Rumble-Rumble.

Thinking about Operation Rumble-Rumble-Rumble

made him think about the canebrake rattlers. He knew that when the sun rose again, he and Bingo would have to figure out a way to acquire some sugar without getting *snip-snap-zip-zapped*. His invisible thinking cap was squeezing his head. Moreover, a queasy feeling gurgled in his belly. Then the gurgling turned into a growl. That made him realize that he was hungry. He and Bingo had gone all day, and now part of the night, without eating. Those crawdads were only a distant memory.

He thought about slipping out to find something, but just as he did, he heard the rain pelting the roof of the car. In times of rain, Information Officers needed to stand by in case of lightning strikes.

He rubbed his tummy. Oh well, he thought. He could wait. He knew if he kept busy, he might forget about his grumbling stomach.

He glanced again at the picture of the armadillo and remembered the strange box underneath the front seat. Maybe, he thought . . . So, he squeezed under there, nose first. Raccoons have extrasensory paws, and soon his felt the hard, metallic box with the spring latch. He pried it open again, but only enough to slip a single paw inside the box.

He reached in, and sure enough, he touched something . . . something hard. It was cool to his touch, and thick, not at all like the art he had found earlier. He tugged on the mys-

tery object, but it got stuck in the opening of the box. It was too thick. He tried to pry open the lid a little more, but the way the box was jammed underneath the seat prevented the lid from opening wide enough to get the hard thick thing out.

He tugged some more.

And some more.

And some *mmmooooorrrrre*!

He finally braced his back feet against the seat and gave a giant *ttttuuuuuugggg*!

Oooomph!

He fell backwards in a furry ball, never letting the odd object out of his possession. He had his prize, right there between his two front paws. The thing was long and flat. It had shiny chrome on the top and bottom and wood in the middle. It had holes on both of the long sides.

Considering the holes, maybe it was a special kind of spyglass? He held it up to look through the holes, but he couldn't see anything. If it was a spyglass, it wasn't very useful. Still, it's the job of a Scout to figure these things out.

All five senses went into action:

1. Sight—He turned it over and over, admiring its shiny chrome plates. He noticed that it had a bunch of curlicues inscribed on those plates, and

little screws on the ends that held the plates to the wood.

2. Smell—Seriously, it was a little musty and dusty. No telling how long it had been in that box.

3. Touch—The metal parts were smooth and cool. The wooden part was also smooth, but not as cool.

4. Taste—He tried biting it. But it was definitely too hard for chewing. He touched it with his tongue. It didn't really have a taste per se, but because of the aforementioned must and dust, it began to tickle his nose, and before he knew it . . . *Aaaachoooo!* And that is when he discovered . . .

5. Sound!

56

AVAILABLE IN TWELVE MAJOR KEYS, THE HOHNER
Marine Band Harmonica was a favorite for blues harp play-
ers of all stripes. Bob Dylan. Bruce Springsteen. Neil Young.
But before all of them, came Snooky Pryor.

According to Audie Brayburn, "Snooky Pryor could blow
the socks off those lightweights." Back in 1949, Bob and
Bruce and Neil were just babies. But when they grew up,
they surely knew about Snooky Pryor, and so did Audie
Brayburn. After listening to Snooky Pryor play his harp,
Audie was determined to learn how to play the blues, so he
bought a Hohner Marine Band Harmonica, key of C major.
Found it in Kresge's in downtown Houston. Lost it in the
Sugar Man Swamp.

57

IT'S SAFE TO SAY THAT WHEN J'MIAH SNEEZED AND heard the resulting noise, he was startled, but not in a bad way. In fact, he was rather charmed by it. In his paws was a . . . a . . . music thingie. J'miah had a genuine music thingie. He gave it another sniff, which resulted in another *Aaachooo!* And sure enough, another note flew out, this one a little higher than the last. He closed his eyes and savored the sound. The purity of the note floated into his ears, and for a moment it lifted him right into the air of the car. His thoughts floated along with him. *First art. And now music.* To J'miah the box underneath the passenger's seat was becoming a source of cultural wonder. Who knew what else he might find in there. Sculpture? Poetry? Film noir?

But while he was basking in his reverie, someone snatched—yes, you heard me, snatched—the music thingie right out of his paws!

Bingo! (Hah, did it again.)

"Mine," said J'miah.

"I just want to try it," said Bingo.

"But I found it first," said J'miah.

Tug.

Whine.

Tug tug.

Whine whine.

Tug tug tug.

At this point, if Little Mama and Daddy-O had been present, it's highly likely that our Scouts would have been relieved of the music thingie until they could shake and make up.

But seeing as how Little Mama and Daddy-O weren't there, the argument went on and on and on, and it might still be going on had it not been for a very loud *ZIP!* A huge bolt of lightning slipped out of the clouds, and *POW!* It hit the ground right next to the old DeSoto. *Sssshhhhh-sssshhhh . . . weee . . . oooooohhhhoooo . . . blip bloop blip . . .* In the same moment that a gush of rain pelted the windshield, the lights on the dash began to glow, and once again the Voice of Intelligence slipped into the humid air of the DeSoto. To the raccoons' surprise, here is what it said: ". . . so come on down to Paradise Pies Café on the Beaten Track Road. You can't buy a finer fried sugar pie, made out of pure canebrake sugar. Yessirree, Bob, those pies will Kick. Your. Booty!"

And with that, the Voice faded, but before it died out, the raccoons heard, "Have a good day and a good idea," followed by a long, deep "Arrrooooo!" All of that was ended with a *click*, and the lights flickered off again.

Bingo and J'miah sat in the silence for a good long while, the music thingie all but forgotten. The Voice had told them many things in the past, things about the weather, about fishing, about the price of corn. And even though the price of corn meant nothing to them, everything the Voice had ever said had been true, including the terrible news about the Farrow Gang. But the Voice had never told them anything about Paradise Pies. Or about kicking booty, either.

What could it all mean? they wondered.

But then Bingo thought about the Sugar Man.

Pies.

Sugar Man.

Pies.

Sugar Man.

Pies. *Made out of pure canebrake sugar.* And all at once, our Information Officer had a good idea. "J'miah," he said, "I think we need some Paradise Pies."

58

SOMEONE ELSE WAS LISTENING TO COYOTEMAN JIM in the middle of the night—Chap and Sweetums. When Chap heard that ad, he grinned from ear to ear.

"Genius," he told the cat.

When people heard that ad, they'd be lined up all the way down Beaten Track Road. Yessirree, Chap just knew it.

"It won't be long now," he told Sweetums. And with that, he rubbed the cat between the ears and turned off the light. "Wait," said Sweetums, "I have something to tell you." But of course the boy paid no heed. Heed cannot be paid if you don't know the language. Chap just rolled over and pulled up the covers.

59

"HOW MUCH LONGER? HOW MUCH LONGER? HOW much longer till canebrake sugar?" the fifteen Farrow hoglets chanted, over and over.

"Not long now, my bad little Farrows," said Clydine, grinding her teeth in annoyance. Then she glared at Buzzie and asked, "Exactly *how* much longer, my dearie dear?" She tapped her cloven hoof in impatience. They had been on the go for a couple of hours, and they didn't seem any nearer to the canebrake than they had when they first woke up.

The chant from the hoglets was driving Clydine mad. She could tolerate bickering and snickering. She could manage head-butting and tusk-tangling. But she absolutely couldn't abide chanting, especially that insidious question that drives all parents mad, "How much longer?"

Buzzie knew that Clydine's skin was getting perilously thin. He tried to calm her with a diversion. "I know," he said. "Let's wallow some more."

He led them all to a shallow pond that normally would

have served as drinking water for a herd of cattle that had vamoosed ahead of the hogs' approach. Buzzie could see that it was the perfect place to stop.

"Yay!" squealed the little Farrows.

"You wallow," said Clydine. "I'm going to go beat my head against a tree." Which is exactly what she did. And while it made Clydine feel so much better, it destroyed the poor tree. By the time she was done beating her head against it, there wasn't a single leaf left on its branches, and all its bark had popped completely off.

Buzzie watched her in admiration. "That's my girl," he said.

And while all fifteen of his piggy brood watched, he did a huge belly flop in the now-mucked-up pond. *Smack!* "Hooray!" they cried.

There were happy hogs aplenty. At least until the smallest one chanted, "How much longer? How much longer?"

60

BINGO AND J'MIAH KNEW THEY WERE RUNNING out of time. They could feel the increasing strength of the *rumble-rumble-rumble-rumble*s.

But it took them a while to figure out where the Paradise Pies Café was actually located. The Voice had said "Beaten Track Road." They had no idea what that meant. They didn't have GPS like Steve had on his lost cell phone, nor did they have a paper napkin map. But they figured it couldn't be too far away, or the Voice wouldn't have brought it up in the first place. So even while the rain continued, the two of them bounded out into the evening.

And they might not ever have found the little café, except that J'miah got tired of going around in large circles and finally stopped to ask a skunk for directions. Skunks get a bad rap for their propensity to spray others with their fowl musk, but their noses are highly regarded. And as long as they weren't scared or angry, they kept their musks to themselves. J'miah figured that a skunk would be able to point them in the direction of the pies just by virtue of his schnoz. The first skunk he saw, he approached very cautiously. The skunk was happy to oblige. The musk alarm was left untripped.

As it turned out, the café wasn't all that far from the DeSoto, maybe only a mile or so. Who knew?

Sure enough, before Bingo and J'miah even saw the sign, their noses started tingling. My, oh my, those pies smelled good. Bingo didn't even have to open his eyes to see that he was on the right track. His mouth watered, and he even drooled a little bit.

J'miah had to shake him out of his trance. "There it is," he said.

Bingo opened his eyes at the same time that the rain finally came to a close. Sure enough, right in front of them, was a small building, sitting up on stilts so that if the water from the nearby Bayou Tourterelle ever came out of its banks, it would just flow right underneath it, no harm done. The building had a front porch and a back porch. There was only one light coming through the windows, and while they stood there, that light went out.

Both of their tummies growled. The sticky air was so thick with the smell of those pies that it seemed like they could practically bite it.

J'miah gave Bingo a nudge. "Don't forget our mission."

"Mission?" asked Bingo. The pie smell had erased all memory.

"Operation Rumble-Rumble-Rumble," J'miah reminded him.

For a second Bingo drooled a little more. Then J'miah gave him a whack on the back.

"Mission, mission, mission," J'miah said.

At last Bingo snapped out of his pie aroma coma.

"Right," he said. "Mission." All at once the urgency of the task in front of him gave him a power surge. He was a Sugar Man Swamp Scout after all. Their mission was to wake up the Sugar Man so that he could deal with the advancing hogs.

Everything depended upon waking up the Sugar Man.

A pie wasn't the same as the actual canebrake sugar, but it had canebrake sugar in it, and since the canebrake sugar was guarded by a whole phalanx of *snipping-snapping-zipping-zapping*, the pie would have to do.

So, here they were, advancing on the café so that they could steal pies, and wouldn't you know it, the side window was barely cracked open. Barely, but enough. By scampering along the thick limb of a japonica bush that leaned against the house and led right to the window, all they had to do was pop off the screen, and *thump*, first Bingo was in, then *thump*, J'miah was in, then *thump*, *thump*, they were both on the counter.

Victory!

It took a minute to reconnoiter, but once their eyes adjusted to their surroundings, they looked around and saw . . . mountains of pies.

Paradise. That's where they were. Paradise.

In fact, they were in Paradise Pies Café.

But they weren't alone.

61

SOMETIME DEEP IN THE DEEPEST MIDDLE OF HIS MID-night nap, Sweetums heard a *thump*. What was that? He cocked his ears. Nothing.

Then he heard it again. *Thump*. There was someone in the café. Was it a rat? He could not believe that a rat would try to enter his domain. No self-respecting rat would dare cross the threshold of Paradise Pies Café, not while Sweetums was in charge of pest control.

Thump.

Big rat, thought Sweetums. He slid off the bed, careful not to make any noise, tiptoed around the corner and over to the door. He crouched down as low as he could, making himself as thin as a shadow. The door between the back of the cabin and the café kitchen was only cracked a tiny bit, just enough for him to poke his nose through.

His whiskers twitched. There was definitely something there, but with his superior sense of smell, he could tell that it was not a rat. It also wasn't a human. Sweetums had smelled plenty of them.

For sure it wasn't a dog. He'd smelled them, too. Disgusting creatures. Plus, dogs were so loud. Whatever was creeping around in the kitchen was being very quiet, and very stealthy.

Thump, thump.

Two. There were two somethings in the kitchen. Sweetums twitched his tail. He crouched a little lower. And then, in the light cast off by the clock radio, he saw two stripy figures walk along the edge of the kitchen counter, one behind the other. As the cat watched, one of the figures paused and sniffed the air. Then they both looked right in his direction. Their terrible black eyes glowered from behind their terrible black masks.

Wait a minute. Black masks? Now Sweetums knew exactly what he was seeing: robbers!

Paradise Pies was being robbed!

"Thieves!" Sweetums' ginger coat suddenly doubled in size. (Even though cats are not in the same family as raccoons, they are equally poofable.) As soon as Sweetums' paws gathered some traction on the wood floor, he darted beneath Chap's bed. There he bunched himself up and let out a low furious growl. In addition, he managed to hiss several times.

"People! Where are you?" he finally cried, in his loudest meow. Weren't the humanoids supposed to protect him from this sort of thing? Shouldn't they take some sort of defensive action? Why would they not wake up?

As it turns out, the people were so tired from cooking pies all day that they were pooped, kaput, sacked out. Some might say "dead to the world." In other words, completely, thoroughly, utterly, sound asleep, with "sound" being the primary descriptor.

62

MEANWHILE, BACK IN THE KITCHEN, BINGO AND J'MIAH knew they had been discovered. They grabbed as many pies as they could. They shoveled pawsful of them out the crack in the kitchen window.

Finally, Bingo whispered to J'miah, "That's good. Let's go!" They had all that they could safely carry, and *thump*, *thump*, out they slid, and away they went as fast as their stripy little legs could carry them.

Pip pip, young pie thieves!

63

It took forever for Sweetums' nerves to settle. Every time he closed his eyes, he could see those sinister black masks. His normally sleek ginger fur stayed poofed out for hours.

First the *rumble-rumble-rumble-rumble*s. Now a home invasion. What next?

He also realized that he needed to use his box, but that was two rooms over, next to the washing machine. He curled into a ball. He could wait.

No way was he getting out from under this bed, not until the sun came up. No way. Nuh-uh. Not going to happen.

64

IT WAS A LONG NIGHT FOR COYOTEMAN JIM, TOO. As soon as he ran the commercial for Paradise Pies, he started getting one call after another. Folks rang in with all sorts of questions:

- Which direction should I take to get there?
  That depends on where you're coming from.
- Where do I turn?
  Follow the signs.
- How much does a pie cost?
  One pie for two dollars. Three pies for five dollars.
- Do they use real muscovado sugar?
  Right out of the canebrake.
- Is the sugar fresh-squeezed?
  Right there in the kitchen.
- Do they have French roast coffee?
  Nope. Community Coffee, roasted in Baton Rouge.

- How many pies can one person eat?

  As many as one person wants.
- Do they have takeout?

  Only if you can get out the door without eating them.

Coyoteman Jim just finished answering one phone call, when it rang again. He could barely even squeeze out time for the weather report amidst all those questions. Sometime after midnight the calls finally slowed down and he was able to catch his breath. He smiled from ear to ear. If that night had been any indication, there was going to be a very large crowd at Paradise Pies Café in the morning. He just hoped there would be a pie left for him!

And then the phone rang again.

Sonny Boy Beaucoup. Coyoteman Jim felt a chill run through the air. But Sonny Boy wasn't calling about pies. Nope. He was calling to let Coyoteman Jim know about the groundbreaking ceremony that he and Jaeger Stitch were planning to hold for the Gator World Wrestling Arena and Theme Park.

"Day after tomorrow," he said. "Be sure to let your listeners know."

Coyoteman Jim crossed his fingers behind his back and said, "Sure thing, Mr. Beaucoup. Sure thing." Then he wrote down all the information, including the guest list. When he got to the mayor's name, his pen mysteriously ran out of ink.

Like we said before, there is some news that is meant to be repeated, and there is some that is not. The news about the groundbreaking ceremony fell into the latter category.

Of course, Coyoteman Jim knew that eventually, word would get out despite his efforts. But in the meantime he'd keep it under his hat as long as he could.

65

RACCOONS ARE FAIRLY DEXTEROUS. THEY CAN WALK on either four legs or two legs. When they're in a hurry, four legs is best. But right then their front paws were full of fried sugar pies, which meant that their only alternative was to run as fast as they could on their back legs.

Which they did.

All the way back to the DeSoto.

Whew!

They scurried in through the entryway on the passenger side and plopped onto the front seat. Since raccoons aren't all that great at counting, we'll just say that they had in their collective paws more than four fried pies and fewer than a dozen. And let us also say that carrying those fried pies right underneath their noses was a kind of delicious torture.

Bingo looked at the pile of pies scattered on the front seat. "I think we took more than we needed," he said.

J'miah nodded. Then he said exactly what Bingo was

thinking. "Since we have so many, I think we could taste at least one of these, don't you?"

Since they were both in agreement, they each picked up a Paradise Pie, and—sit down, brothers and sisters—they did not think they had ever tasted anything so rapturous in their entire lives. Not crawdads. Not blackberries. Not crickets. Not slugs. Not minnows. Nothing could compare.

Those pies kicked their stripy booties!

They ate one pie each. Then just one more. Then *really* just one more. Okay, this was it, absolutely only *one* more.

Bingo and J'miah were in Paradise Pie delectation. But then a tiny voice in Bingo's head sang out, "Stop!"

His belly pooched out like a balloon.

"Oh, my!" said J'miah. He looked down at his own belly. It was covered in crumbs, and it also pooched out. He had never felt so full.

But it wasn't really the bellies that were the problem. In a panic Bingo patted the seat. He looked underneath it. He jumped into the backseat. He patted the floorboard. He checked the dashboard. He even stood on the rear dash. At last he had to force himself to look back at the front seat, to the spot where all the stolen pies were supposed to be, the pies that they needed to lure the Sugar Man out of his sleeping lair, the pies that were supposed to substitute for the canebrake sugar. The pies that he and J'miah had gobbled up. Those pies. They were gone.

Almost.

There, all by its little lonesome, was the last fried pie.

One.
　　Fried.
　　　　Pie.
　　　　　　All.
　　　　　　　　Alone.
　　　　　　　　　　On.
　　　　　　　　　　　　The.
　　　　　　　　　　　　　　Front.
　　　　　　　　　　　　　　　　Seat.

And if that wasn't bad enough . . . *rumble-rumble-rumble-rumble* . . . *rumble-rumble-rumble-rumble*!

In their pie-eating frenzy, our Scouts had momentarily forgotten about the Farrow Gang! Bingo slapped his forehead. Here they were, trying to be good little Scouts, and they had acted like . . . well, like hogs! And not only that, but now they only had one pie for the Sugar Man. One tiny little sugar pie.

What to do?

Rumble-rumble-rumble-rumble.

J'miah brushed his paws together to get the sugar off them.

Bingo looked through the DeSoto's now-shiny windows. Through the vines, he could tell the sun was on the rise. There was no going back to Paradise Pies Café in the daylight.

He sat back on the seat. Beside him J'miah squinted. His invisible cap pressed down on his eyebrows. Then he busied himself by combing the remaining crumbs off the leather-covered bench. Every so often he paused and admired the art on the dashboard. The armadillo made him feel just a little better, but not much.

It could have been a total doomsday scenario, except that Bingo opened his mouth and . . . *BURP!* A sugary belch floated through the air. Followed by another *burpburpburp.*

Before they knew it, the air was filled with the smell of sugar. It was small comfort, because soon enough the seriousness of their situation settled in.

The facts were these: (1) they were supposed to gather up some raw cane sugar to wake up the Sugar Man; (2) they were blocked by the canebrake rattlers; (3) the Voice had told them that the Paradise Pies would kick booty; (4) surely a Paradise Pie would wake up the Sugar Man; (5) we'll put the emphasis on *a* pie, as in *one* pie.

The two brothers looked at the single fried pie. Would

one pie be enough? Enough for a creature whose hands were as big as palmettos, whose feet were the size of canoes? Enough for a guy who kept *Crotalus horridus GIGANTICUS* as a pet? Bingo's tuft stood straight up between his ears. J'miah squinted.

One pie would have to do it.

And with the sun in the corner of the sky, Bingo gathered up that single pie, and together he and J'miah crossed their fingers and toes. Then they headed back out, back to the deepest, darkest part of the forest.

Rumble-rumble-rumble-rumble . . .

The Third Day

66

CHAP PADDED INTO THE KITCHEN. HE COULD hear his mother pushing chairs under tables, getting the café ready for the day. He looked at the clock—4:30 a.m. The numbers glowed in the dim light. The sun would be up soon. He switched on the radio.

Into the quiet air of the kitchen, Coyoteman Jim's resonant voice slipped out. He was just signing off, "Have a good day and a good idea."

Chap reached for a bag of coffee beans and poured them into the grinder. As he poured the water into the coffeemaker, he saw something odd, something unusual, something he'd never seen before in the kitchen . . . muddy paw prints. He looked closer at the prints and followed them to the windowsill. The radio was there. Steve's cell phone was there. The window screen was missing. He looked back at the counters. Pies. Lots of pies. All stacked up.

But . . . not as many as there were when he went to bed.

"Thieves," he cried. "We've been robbed!"

And in that same instant Coyoteman Jim cut loose with his final, "Arrooooooo!"

67

WHAT WOULD GRANDPA AUDIE DO? THAT WAS THE question that rang through Chap's head as he looked at the muddy paw prints on the counter. Chap knew that Audie had always liked the local raccoons. But at the moment "like" was not the word he would associate with them.

He might have considered shooting at them if he'd had a gun. Or at least shooting over their heads to scare them. But he didn't have a gun. All he had was his grandfather's old machete, and it was strictly used for chopping sugarcane, not for dispatching wildlife.

"We live on their land," Grandpa Audie had always told Chap. "Not the other way around." And Chap respected that. Thinking about his grandpa made him calm down a little. If Audie were still alive, he would likely have turned the robbery into a funny story. Chap thought about his grandpa's drawing of the raccoon with the harmonica.

But Grandpa Audie did not have to raise a boatload of

cash in order to keep Jaeger Stitch and Sonny Boy Beaucoup from transforming the swamp into a freak show.

Grandpa Audie was not the man of the household now. Chap was. Or at least he was supposed to be. While Grandpa Audie was busy meeting his Maker, raccoons had been busy stealing pies. And Chap had not prevented either of those events from occurring. He wanted to kick something. Throw something. Hit something. And all those somethings looked like . . . raccoons!

But he also knew that his grandfather would never have kicked, thrown, or hit anything, including pie thieves.

As Chap looked around, he realized what he needed right then was . . . coffee! He filled the GBH mug to the very rim. His hands shook as he raised it to his lips.

Hot hot hot.

Bitter bitter bitter.

The jet-black brew was not getting any better. He swallowed, then took another sip. Then, without waiting for his mother, he cleaned the counter, wiping away all the evidence. He looked at the mountain of pies they had baked. Dozens and dozens. The result of hours spent chopping the cane, squeezing the thick stalks in the juicer, rolling the dough, mixing up the filling, and then frying everything in deep, deep oil, at a very high temperature. It had been a lot of work. And now, there were stacks of fresh fried pies, sitting on their counter. He counted them.

Result: The raccoons had taken more than four, he figured, but fewer than a dozen. Chap could see that there were plenty of pies left. More than enough. Boo-coos of pies. Pies to the sky.

Nevertheless, "A man's house is his castle," said Chap, and even though no great harm had been done, the castle had been breached. Measures would have to be taken to be sure that the raccoons did not cross the moat again. And he knew exactly what those measures would be.

"Traps!" A few years back, a young bobcat had set up housekeeping under the porch, and Grandpa Audie had caught it in his Havahart trap, then carried it far down the bayou, where he set it free. They had never seen that bobcat again.

Chap could do the same with the raccoons. No guns needed. He puffed out his chest. No hairs needed either.

He took another sip of the dark coffee. It burned his tongue. How did anyone ever come to like this stuff? He started to ask that question out loud, but before he could, his mother's voice interrupted him. "Chap?" she said. "Would you come here, please?" He turned toward her as she opened the door.

There, on the front porch, stood a very long line of

people, hungry-for-sugar-pie people. Chap had never seen such a long line. It started at the door and snaked all the way past the parking lot and out to the Beaten Track Road. Mom turned the sign over from CLOSED to OPEN and said, "Y'all come in." And they did. In droves.

As fast as he could, Chap served up pies. He had never seen so many chops being licked or heard so many compliments.

They'd take a bite and say, "Mmmmm . . . these pies sure enough kick booty!"

One-dollar bills. Five-dollar bills. Ten-dollar bills. Even a couple of two-dollar bills. One by one, the customers walked through the door and ordered pies. And bill by bill, the boat began to fill up too. It wasn't long before the bottom was covered in cash. And Paradise Pies Café was completely out of fried sugar pies.

68

LET ME TELL YOU, THERE ARE MANY KINDS OF SUGAR. There is the sugar that comes from beets. There is the sugar that comes from corn. But the wild sugarcane that grows along the banks of the Bayou Tourterelle produces the finest sugar of all.

Muscovado. That's what it's called. No one really knows how the first plants got here, seeing as how it's not native to Texas at all. Maybe a seed blew in on a storm. Maybe a passing trader planted a batch. Maybe a goose deposited a seed as it flew by. Regardless of how or why it arrived, the muscovado sugar is one of the swamp's best mysteries.

It's not grainy like the white sugar you buy in the supermarket. No, no, no. In its raw state, it's brown, like the sand in Barbados, like the water of the Bayou Tourterelle, like the feathers of a roadrunner. Brown like that.

It tastes like heaven.

There's nothing like it. Nothing. And Clydine wanted some. Snort, snort, snort! Get that girl some muscovado!

69

WITH THE SUN MOVING ACROSS THE MIDDLE OF THE sky, Bingo knew they had to pick up their pace. They would need every bit of light that the daytime sun could offer as they made their way through the darkest part of the swamp.

Hurry, Scouts, hurry! As if to prove the point, *rumble-rumble-rumble-rumble*, he could feel the hogs coming closer.

Then Bingo had a horrible thought. Even if the pie did wake up the Sugar Man, what would happen then? Scout orders were, "Wake up the Sugar Man." They didn't say what to do next.

Have we forgotten the stuff about *the wrath of the Sugar Man*?

Nosirree, Bob. We most decidedly have not. After all, we remember that the Sugar Man had that wee bit of rattlesnake venom in his blood, and rattlesnakes, as everyone knows, are feisty. In fact, they're downright venomous. *Snip-snap-zip-zap.*

Take heed, Scouts. Take heed.

70

THE SOUNDER NORMALLY DIDN'T TRAVEL DURING daylight hours, but everyone had become so impatient that Buzzie made an executive decision to hit the trail early. That did not mollify the irascible Clydine. Instead of praising him for his ambition, she was a bundle of complaints.

Clearly, she had not gotten her beauty rest, and it showed. Her yellow eyes were yellower than ever, and her curly tail drooped. What had he ever seen in her? Buzzie wondered.

She wasn't the only one who complained. Every single little porker in the pod had some injustice to report.

"He pulled my tail."

"She bumped me."

"I need to use the restroom."

"I've got a bellyache."

It was constant. If only hogs could climb a wall, Buzzie would have climbed one.

Sugar. Just get us to the sugar, he prayed. And with a

snort, he told his clan, "We're almost there." But they had heard that before, so they just kept complaining.

"He's got my ear in his mouth."

"I want another mud bath."

"You're not the boss of me."

Buzzie wanted to drop all of them off at the nearest hog shelter. Of course, that would require a hog shelter, which to our knowledge does not exist.

That's when the porcine divine intervened and they rumbled up to an enormous round hay bale.

"Attack!" snorted Buzzie. And all seventeen of our grouchy grunters lowered their heads and charged the unsuspecting hay bale. There are reports that hay rained down in four states. But the important thing was that tempers were assuaged. Clydine regained her composure. And Buzzie was a semi-happy camper.

71

CHAP WAS ALSO A SEMI-HAPPY CAMPER. THE SIGHT OF all that cash settling into the bottom of the boat made him think they had a chance of keeping the café. But even if they managed to save the café, Chap knew that what they really needed to save was the swamp itself. Sonny Boy's voice echoed in his head. *If I see some proof of the Sugar Man, I'll give you the whole darned swamp.*

But proof? Of the Sugar Man? All he had was his grandpa's old drawing, the one that had been stuck to the back of the raccoon-with-the-harmonica picture. A drawing with the date: 1949.

That date always reminded Chap of the DeSoto. Then Chap realized that if he couldn't save the swamp, the ivory-bill wouldn't be the only thing lost forever. The other thing would be the chance of ever finding his grandfather's prized Sportsman with the Simplimatic transmission and the waterfall grille.

"It even had a hood ornament that lit up whenever the

lights came on," his grandpa had told him. "There was no other car like it." Chap knew that it had been one of his grandfather's deepest wishes to find that car, right along with his other wish, to see the ivory-bill one more time and add it at last to his sketchbook.

And just like it had always been for Chap, Grandpa Audie's deepest wishes were his own deepest wishes. *Nosotros somos paisanos.* We are fellow countrymen. We come from the same soil. Grandpa Audie was gone, but his wishes were still there, smack dab in the middle of Chap's heart. If he could go search for the bird and the car right then, he would. Except, the complete sellout of pies meant that there were still hours of work in front of him.

"We have to double up," his mother said.

So while the hogs were attacking the hay bale, Chap attacked the sugarcane. Soon, his arms ached. His back ached. His whole body ached. Not only that, but the afternoon sun was relentless. He wiped his face on his sleeve, but that didn't give him much relief, considering that his sleeves were wet with his own sweat.

He also knew that the rattlesnakes could wake up at any moment. Grandpa Audie had warned him, "Don't try to use the lullaby more than once a day. It won't work." Chap had never asked him what would happen. He had a pretty good idea.

Once again, he bundled the stalks up and tied them with twine, and started pulling his double-heavy bundle up the trail. He had to pull it with both hands behind his back, which made him lean low to the ground. He felt the muscles in his thighs strain at the weight. Sweat dripped off his nose. He had to breathe through his mouth to get enough air, and his side ached to boot.

And maybe because his face was so close to the dirt, he spied the tracks. There, in the soft mud. Raccoon tracks. He dropped his load and sat down hard. His chest rose and fell with the deep breaths he had to take. Then he rubbed his hand over the tracks. They were fresh, less than a day old.

Had the same raccoons that had made the tracks on their kitchen counter made these, too? He leaned closer to get a better look. He could see that there were two of them, side by side. A pair. Just like in the kitchen. Judging from the sharp turn these tracks made in the mud, it looked like they had come to a rapid stop, done a one-eighty, and hightailed it back in the direction from which they had come.

"The rattlers," said Chap. "They must have had a close encounter with the rattlers."

But what were they doing at the canebrake anyways? Most critters knew to stay away from the snakes. Had the raccoons come for the same reason he had? For sugar? And then another question popped into his head: Since when had the local raccoons developed such a sweet tooth? Especially when there was an abundance of local food? The swamp had plenty of crawdads and berries and slugs and lizards, all the main stuff of a raccoon diet.

Chap scratched his head. One thing was for certain. If those raccoons had, in fact, become sugar fiends, then he'd definitely have to set the traps. Because the other thing he knew: Once raccoons discovered a cache of something they loved, they'd return. Oh, yes, they would.

72

BUT RIGHT NOW LET'S RETURN TO THE FACTS IF WE can. The overall weight of the 1949 DeSoto Sportsman was more than thirty-five hundred pounds. It had a width of 125.5 inches and a total length of 17 feet.

That's a lot of car, my homies.

But what, you might be asking, are the dimensions of Sonny Boy Beaucoup's superstretch Hummer limousine, the one that Leroy shined until he could see himself in its slick black surface?

According to our expert, Phil at LA Custom Coaches, it was quite a bit wider than the DeSoto, coming in at one hundred eighty inches, and twice as long—thirty-five feet. Where it really had an advantage, however, was in the weight category. The Hummer clocked in at close to eleven thousand pounds. Whoa baby, that is one solid piece of car flesh.

Then again, part of its girth was due to the fact that it had a full bar set up, with neon and strobe lighting, three plasma television sets, and seating for twenty-four. In other words, it was like a rolling party room.

73

DID WE SAY THAT THE SUPERSTRETCH HUMMER seated twenty-four? Why, yes. Yes, we did. This meant that Sonny Boy and Jaeger decided to invite twenty-two dignitaries for the ground breaking. The plan was to gather at the Beaucoups' Homestead for lunch on the veranda, during which Jaeger would display her alligator wrestling skills.

Afterwards, Leroy would drive the entire party to the site of the ground breaking.

Oh, did we also tell you that the site of the ground breaking was along the banks of the Bayou Tourterelle, where the canebrake grew? And that everyone in the party would have to walk past Paradise Pies Café to get there? Why, no, I don't believe we did.

Sonny Boy rubbed his hands together in glee.

"We might as well have fried pie while we're there." He chuckled. And once again, Jaeger sort of wanted to kiss him, an urge that made her feel somewhat sick to her stomach.

As if he were reading her mind, he asked, "You *will* do that alligator kissing trick, won't you?"

"Of course," she replied. Kissing the alligator was all part of her wrestling routine. She had kissed hundreds of alligators. Kissing an alligator instead of Sonny Boy Beaucoup made her feel quite a bit better.

For his part, Sonny Boy had no desire to kiss Jaeger Stitch. He'd just as soon kiss the Sugar Man.

Hah!

There was not one iota of evidence that the Sugar Man actually existed. Absolutely no documented proof. He was just as mythical as Barmanou and Sasquatch and the Yeti. The only person who ever claimed to see him was his ancient sea-faring grandfather. And Alouicious? He was just a memory too.

Just like the woodpecker. Just like his father, Quenton.

Just like Audie Brayburn. Just crazy old memories. That's all.

74

AUDIE BRAYBURN WASN'T JUST A CRAZY OLD MEMORY to his daughter, or his grandson, Chap. Nor was he a crazy old memory to his friend Coyoteman Jim. Even the cat remembered him.

And here's something I'll bet you didn't know: Audie wasn't just a crazy old memory to the Sugar Man either. Nope.

75

FROM TIME TO TIME, NOT VERY OFTEN ACTUALLY, but still . . . the Sugar Man woke up of his own accord, just to mosey down to the canebrake and chew on that delicious muscovado sugar.

He might have enjoyed the company of one of his cousins, Barmanou or Sasquatch or the Yeti, but he knew that it was risky enough having one cryptid (look it up) in a forest, never mind two or more. The cousins were aware of this too, so they all pretty much stayed in their own habitats.

So, imagine how surprised the Sugar Man was one afternoon, oh, sixty-something years back, while he was munching on some sugarcane and singing his rattler lullaby, when he heard an odd noise accompanying the song. He sang it again.

Rock-a-by, oh canebrake rattlers
Sleepy bayou, rock-a-by oh

Canebrake rattlers

Sssslleeeepp.

And the noise played along. It was a noise he liked. It was so much better than that cursed concertina that the pirates played. The Sugar Man raised his head out of the tall cane, and came nose to nose with none other than a young Audie Brayburn, playing his Hohner Marine Band Harmonica, key of C major.

"Howdy," said Audie. Well, the Sugar Man was so surprised, he accidentally swallowed a huge chunk of sugarcane and started coughing and coughing. Audie could see that the tall man was turning bright red, even underneath all of his fur.

Quick as a rabbit, Audie grabbed a nearby branch and *whack!* Smacked him right on the back. The Sugar Man kept right on coughing, and so *whack!* Audie smacked him again.

Just about the time that Gertrude was about to go all *snip-snap-zip-zap* on Audie for whacking her best beloved, out of the Sugar Man's mouth popped the big chunk of cane. It splashed right into the Bayou Tourterelle.

"Whew!" exclaimed the Sugar Man. Then he looked down at Audie, and right there a friendship was struck. For the next several hours, those two chewed cane and also chewed the fat. And if that weren't enough, they both sang

at the top of their lungs. They sang so much that Gertrude got all dreamy and took a keen liking to Audie too.

But soon enough, the Sugar Man got sleepy, so he waved good-bye to Audie, wished him well in his search for the ivory-billed woodpecker, and trekked back to his deep, dark lair.

When the Sugar Man stretched out on his mat, he felt as cozy as could be, knowing that he had a new friend. It was sweet dreams, Sugar Man. And Gertrude was happy too. She curled up right next to him and sssssighed.

Of course, the Swamp Scouts (who were, at that time, the great-greater-greatest ancestors to Bingo and J'miah) kept an eye on the whole thing. Nothing gets by them, nothing at all.

So, a few nights later, when the rain came pouring down in heavy sheets, when Audie was asleep inside the DeSoto, burning up with fever, and his car started to float into the muddy depths of the bayou without him knowing it, the Official Sugar Man Swamp Scouts were alarmed. First, they knocked on the windows of the car and tried to get Audie to wake up. Then they jumped up and down on the roof. Still no movement from inside the car. They even tried to open the doors. They tugged and tugged and pulled and pulled. But Audie had locked the car up tight.

This, they knew, was an emergency. Only one thing to

do! They hurried to the deepest, darkest part of the swamp and implored Gertrude to wake up the Sugar Man. At first, he was sure enough cranky, but once he understood that his new friend Audie was about to be washed downstream, he rushed to the scene, grabbed the back bumper of that DeSoto, and pulled the huge Sportsman away from the edge of the water. Then he plopped it atop a little knoll along the banks of the bayou, where it's sat ever since, hidden, the bust of the old conquistador gazing at the water as it flows on by.

Before the Sugar Man left, he peeked through the windows of the car to make sure that Audie was all right. Just as he did, a small bolt of lightning flashed in his face and momentarily made him see red spots. He blinked. Audie was safe. That was what mattered.

Since then, the Sugar Man has slept longer and longer every year. He's gotten harder and harder to wake up. Just ask Gertrude.

But now? The Farrow Gang was headed their way. If anything counted as an emergency, this was it. Bingo and J'miah knew it. They also knew that if they couldn't wake up the Sugar Man, the Farrow Gang would destroy the swamp for sure.

Bingo held the pie up to his nose. His worries grew. This pie was all that stood between the beautiful Sugar Man Swamp and total destruction.

Say it, sisters and brothers—lives were at stake.

The Fourth Night

76

SPEAKING OF HOGS . . .

Rumble-rumble-rumble-rumble.

From the deepest, darkest part of the swamp, Gertrude uncoiled herself and shook her impressive rattle, *chichichi-chichi.* If only all that rattling could scare away the pervasive fleas! She itched from stem to stern.

It made her a little cranky. In fact, it made her a little *snippy-snappy-zippy-zappy.* Those biting fleas made her want to bite something, maybe even something furry.

77

OKAY, NOW WE'RE *REALLY* SPEAKING OF HOGS. . . .

"I'm starving!" Clydine snorted.

"Me too." Buzzie snorted.

"Us too." The Farrow Gang snorted.

All seventeen members of the Gang stood up and looked around. They had made such a mess of the hay bale that they decided to relocate to a nearby watering hole and do some major big-time wallowing.

And when they were done with their wallowing, they found a century-old pecan tree, one that had been standing next to that now-destroyed watering hole for, well, a century. Those hogs head-butted the tree until its pecans came pouring down. They mashed those pecans up so much that they turned them into pecan butter.

All of this was accompanied by a great deal of squealing and oinking. It was sheer bedlam, followed by a whole lot of huffing and puffing.

Yowzers!

78

Bingo and J'miah crept into the outskirts of the Sugar Man's deep, dark lair. There wasn't exactly a door to knock on or a bell to ring. They looked all around for Gertrude, but didn't see her anywhere.

"Where is she?" asked Bingo.

It seems like a huge guard rattlesnake would be hard to miss, but despite their superior eyesight, earsound, and nosesmell, neither Bingo nor J'miah could detect her.

"I've got a bad feeling about this," said J'miah. Gertrude had told them that she didn't eat furry things, but could a rattlesnake be trusted?

Hmmm . . . Gertrude had also told them to fetch some canebrake sugar, but had she given them the rattlesnake lullaby? No, she most definitely had not.

She was supposed to guard the Sugar Man. But was she in her guard post position? Again, that would be a negative.

Our raccoons were in a conundrum, sports fans.

Then Bingo got an idea. He handed the fried pie to J'miah and said, "Here. I'm going up." And with that, he scampered up a large magnolia tree. "Maybe I can see better from up here."

"B-b-be careful," stammered J'miah, holding on to the fried pie. The aroma of it was so lovely that it seemed like it might be a comfort, but was it? We can say with certainty that it was not. J'miah watched as his brother grew smaller and smaller as he scaled the huge tree.

Meanwhile, Bingo finally found a branch that was sturdy enough to crawl out on and look down. He had to use J'miah's trick of squinting in order to see in the darkness. In the shadows, he could detect an arbor of vines and limbs that made up the opening to the Sugar Man's lair. He squinted some more. Directly beneath him was his brother. From Bingo's altitude in the magnolia, J'miah looked very small. But sneaking up behind him was something very large.

Gertrude!

Bingo gulped. "Climb!" he yelled to J'miah. "Climb, climb, climb!"

J'miah looked over his shoulder and heard this unmistakable sound: *CHICHICHICHI!* In that split second of extreme panic, J'miah tossed the fried pie into the air and scooted up that tree as fast as he could.

Had he ever climbed a tree before? No.

Was he afraid of heights? Yes.

Did the whole notion make him queasy? Absolutely.

Did that stop him? No, it did not. His dormant inner climber woke up. He didn't miss a single beat, just pulled himself up, paw over paw, stripy leg after stripy leg, until he trembled right next to his brother.

And while both of them sat there, looking down, they watched in horror as Gertrude swallowed down the single fried pie, the fried pie that Bingo and J'miah had stolen, the fried pie that was supposed to wake up the Sugar Man so that he could scare away the Farrow Gang and save the swamp from certain devastation.

That fried pie.

It was now in the belly of the beast.

And what did the beast have to say?

"Oopssss."

79

OF COURSE, THERE WERE MORE FRIED PIES WHERE that one came from. They just weren't in the possession of the Sugar Man Swamp Scouts. Rather, they were in the kitchen of Paradise Pies Café. And Chap was determined to protect them from invading raccoons.

The Havahart trap that Grandpa Audie had used on the bobcat was just the right size for catching a raccoon. Plus, it was easy to set. The only problem was that there were two raccoons, and only one trap.

It would have to do. Chap figured he'd catch them one at a time.

First, he dragged it out of the boat shed, where it had been stored. Then he sprayed it off with water from the hose so as to eliminate any leftover bobcat musk.

Finally, he sprinkled some of Sweetums' cat food into the back of it and carefully set the trap door.

"There," he said.

He stepped away and, using the hose again, sprayed the

ground on either side of the trap so as to lessen his own scent.

"That ought to do it," he said, admiring the simple engineering of the trap. He wiped his wet hands on the back of his jeans. Then he said, "No animals will be harmed in the protecting of these pies."

80

MEANWHILE, DEEP IN THE DARKEST PART OF THE swamp, Gertrude was feeling a tiny bit of remorse for gobbling up the fried pie, but not too much, because . . .

(1) that pie had kicked her booty! She thought it was the most delicious thing she had ever eaten, but more important . . .
(2) it seemed like the pie had kicked the fleas' booties too, because as soon as she ate it, the fleas stopped biting and went on their merry ways.

The swamp is full of mysteries, and here was a new one. But there was no mystery about how aggravated Bingo and J'miah were with Gertrude.

"Now what?" shouted Bingo from their branch in the magnolia tree.

"Sssssssorrry," said Gertrude, even though she wasn't too sorry. She was vastly relieved to have some respite from those fleas. It was too bad that the silly raccoons had only brought *one* pie. If they'd brought more, they wouldn't be in this pickle at all, would they? She was just about to say, "Ssssayonara, Sssssscouts!" when *rumble-rumble-rumble-rumble.*

"What wassss that?" she asked.

"HOGS!" shouted Bingo and J'miah. Had they not told her this before? Yes! We believe they had.

Rumble-rumble-rumble-rumble.

Bingo and J'miah knew that if they could feel the rumbles all the way into the deepest, darkest part of the swamp, the Farrow Gang was closer than ever. As if to prove the point . . . *rumble-rumble-rumble-rumble.*

"We have to wake up the Sugar Man!" said Gertrude.

Bingo and J'miah both slapped their foreheads. "How?" they asked. "We don't have any sugarcane because *somebody* forgot to mention that the sugarcane is guarded by a whole brigade of vicious rattlesnakes. And now we don't have a sugar pie because *somebody* gobbled it down." They didn't add "like a hog," even though Bingo was tempted.

Gertrude hiccupped. She had to admit that they were in a predicament. It really was too bad that there wasn't any more sugar on hand, either raw or in pie form.

But she did have one secret weapon up her sleeve: *snip-snap-zip-zap.*

"Follow me," she told the Scouts.

From their branch in the magnolia, the raccoon brothers looked at each other. Then they looked down at Gertrude. She hiccupped again. They were having a trust issue here. But alas, did they have any recourse? We can say with certitude that they did not. Tossing their hesitations into the wet swampy air, they scooted backwards down the tree and followed Gertrude past the arbor that marked the entrance, and straight into the den of the Sugar Man, first cousin to Barmanou, second cousin to Sasquatch, third cousin to the Yeti.

It was a death-defying moment in Swamp Scout history.

81

EVEN THOUGH THE NIGHT WAS WANING, AND THE sun was on the verge of popping up, Bingo and J'miah blinked to adjust their vision to the deeper darkness of the inner lair. They looked all around. It wasn't as cozy as their DeSoto, but it had a certain homey feel to it. J'miah scanned the walls. He didn't see any art hanging on them, but he admired the intricate weaving of the vines and branches that created this secret den and kept its inhabitants hidden from the rest of the world.

And of course, right in front of them was the large, sleeping form of the Sugar Man. Bingo and J'miah squeezed next to each other for support. They looked him over from head to toes. It was true. His hands were as large as palmetto ferns. His feet were like small boats. And he was furry all over, like a big bear.

They watched as Gertrude slithered up beside him. "I can give him jussst a sssmall *sssnip-sssnap-zip-zap* right on hisss nossse. That will wake him up."

Bingo and J'miah just nodded. But then Gertrude added, "Of coursssse, rattlesssnake bitesss sssometimess make him . . . Hmmm . . . What isss the word? . . . Oh, yesss. It sssometimesss makesss him . . . *wrathful*. I'm just sssaying."

Bingo shivered. "Do you think it's a good idea?" he asked.

"Do you have another one?" asked Gertrude. But she'd hardly finished her question when . . . from deep inside her gullet . . . *BUURRRPPP!*

"My," she said, but then it happened again . . . *BURRRRPPPP!*

Suddenly the air filled up with the sweet aroma of sugar. Canebrake sugar. Muscovado. And while Bingo and J'miah stood there, the Sugar Man said, in a soft, sweet voice, "Yummmm . . . sugar . . ." And after more than sixty years of sleeping, the Sugar Man sat up, yawned, and stretched.

He blinked several times, twisted his enormous torso to get the kinks out, wiggled his huge toes, and yawned once more. He smiled and patted Gertrude, who, we swear, started purring. "Morning," he said. That's when he noticed Bingo and J'miah.

"Scouts!" he said, a tiny edge of alarm in his voice. "Is there an emergency?"

But Bingo and J'miah didn't even have to answer, because just then . . .

RUMBLE-RUMBLE-RUMBLE-RUMBLE!

82

CLYDINE STUCK HER SNOUT INTO THE AIR. "BUZZIE! Buzzie! What's that I smell?"

Buzzie stuck his snout into the air, "Sugar, m'lovie dovie covey."

At last! Every single hair in Clydine's nose tingled. Oh, the ecstasy. Ah, the euphoria. Her smell buds were in odor exaltation. Her taste buds were dancing atop her tongue. Every cell in her porcine body was in a state of sucrose rapture.

Oh, yes, lift your voices and say it. Say it out loud . . .

"Sugar!" shouted the fifteen junior members of the Farrow Gang.

Yes, it was true. The sweet aroma of the wild sugarcane that grew along the banks of the Bayou Tourterelle was now within the hogs' smelling range.

"I want me some of that wild sugar." Clydine snorted.

"Me too." Buzzie snorted.

"We want sugar." The Farrows snorted.

And with that the seventeen porkers squealed at the tops of their lungs, *"WHHHEEEEEEEE—OOOOOHHHH—WWWWWWWEEEEE—OOOOHHH!"*

The Fourth Day

83

IN A DIFFERENT PART OF THE SWAMP, JAEGER STITCH sat on the hood of the superstretch Hummer while Leroy motored it down to the edge of the Bayou Tourterelle. The big day had arrived for the groundbreaking ceremony, and Jaeger needed a fresh gator.

Attached to the back of the Hummer was a large trailer. It resembled one of the cars that you might see on a circus train. In fact, it even had JAEGER STITCH—WORLD CHAMPION GATOR WRESTLER OF THE NORTHERN HEMISPHERE stenciled on the side, along with a portrait of an enormous gator.

From his spot behind the steering wheel, Leroy thought Jaeger resembled a giant hood ornament. If she had wings on her back, she could be a life-size replica of the Rolls-Royce angel.

Leroy grimaced. Jaeger Stitch was no angel.

She looked over her shoulder at him through the windshield and motioned with her hand for him to slow down. Then she called to him to turn the car around so that the back of the trailer faced the water, no easy feat, considering the Hummer's length. Thirty-five feet, remember? Plus fifteen more for the trailer. Then she told him to turn the headlights off and get out of the car.

Getting out of the car was not something that Leroy had planned to do. But when Jaeger reached through the window and wrapped her hand around his neck, he didn't have a choice. He got out of the car.

He briefly thought about falling on his knees and begging for mercy, but before he could prostrate himself, she grabbed him by the collar and handed him the end of a rope. "Here," she said. "When I say pull, pull." He had no other choice but to do as he was told. Then he looked out at the bayou. He could see a dozen sets of alligator eyes, just on the surface of the water. His knees started to shake. He had never been so close to an alligator before, not to mention a dozen alligators. Wild alligators.

While he stood there, Jaeger Stitch went into action. In her hands she had a long pole with a point on the end. It wasn't a spear, but Leroy thought it could be used as a spear if she had that inclination. He rubbed his neck where Jaeger had so recently grabbed it. As he stood holding his end of the rope, he watched Jaeger uncoil her end. That was when he noticed that there was a chicken tied to it, which she set on the banks of the bayou. (No, not a live chicken. A barbecued chicken.) Then she gave the rope a little tug and climbed atop the trailer.

Leroy figured it out. With the rope in his hand, he was "fishing" for an alligator. Okay, then. All righty. His instinct was to head for the hills, but are there any hills in the swamp? We think you can answer that question all by yourself. Poor Leroy was stuck.

"When I say pull, pull," Jaeger said again. Leroy nodded.

He looked at the quiet water. All he could see were those dozen sets of eyes. Worse, he could tell that they were getting closer and closer to the bank. Since he knew that their eyes were attached to their bodies, he also knew that the alligators were getting ready to dock.

Sure enough, the biggest alligator in the pod swam up to the barbecue chicken. Like that, the beast opened his massive jaws. Leroy had never seen so many teeth in one place in his entire life.

Just as those mighty jaws were about to snap up the chicken, Jaeger yelled, "Pull!" Leroy tugged the rope so hard, it caused the chicken to bounce away.

SNAP! Leroy just about jumped out of his skin. The alligator missed the chicken, but the aroma of barbecue was strong in its nostrils. Leroy watched in astonishment as Jaeger prodded the beast with her pointed stick. The gator moved forward again. "Pull," yelled Jaeger. *SNAP!* Each time the gator tried to *SNAP* the chicken, Jaeger yelled, "Pull." And with each pull and *SNAP*, the gator got closer to the trailer. Ahh, now Leroy could see what she was doing. As soon as the gator climbed into the trailer, Jaeger would slam the gate shut, and voilà! She'd have her victim.

SNAP! SNAP! SNAP!

The problem was, as the gator got closer to the trailer, it also got closer to Leroy. And it seemed to Leroy, although he was no alligator psychologist, that the beast was getting increasingly angry at the ever-moving chicken. Soon, he figured, he'd run out of rope and there would be only a barbecued chicken between him and the alligator.

Just as Leroy was beginning to think that the gator might give up on the chicken and have him for dinner instead, Jaeger grabbed the chicken, threw it into the trailer, poked the gator in just the right spot so that it climbed right into the trailer, and *slam*, she closed the back of the trailer.

Leroy watched as she punched her fist into the air. Then she looked right at him and said, "Go!" And despite his shaking knees, he dropped the rope, bounded behind the steering wheel, and took off. The Hummer's tires dug into the soft dirt of the marsh and made deep ruts as Leroy hit the gas. He wanted to get back to the Homestead as quickly as he could. He was done with alligator hunting.

His heart was beating against his rib cage like a rabbit on

the run. The trees all around him suddenly looked like tall bearded spirits. He'd never seen anything quite so ghostly, at least not until . . . *EEEK!*

First one foot, then another, then two legs, then an entire body . . . slid down the outside of the windshield. Jaeger! Oh my stars! Jaeger! He had forgotten to wait for her to climb into the car. She must have died and had now come back to haunt him.

But wait. No. A ghost wouldn't be so . . . so . . . so *solid.* Would it?

Somehow, when Leroy took off, Jaeger Stitch had managed to leap onto the back of the trailer, jump onto the top of the Hummer, run along all thirty-five feet from back to front, and then slide down the windshield.

And for the second time in this story, someone else, namely Leroy, said, "Oops."

The good news for Leroy was that Jaeger Stitch was not angry with him for this small transgression. Nope. She wasn't thinking at all about Leroy. The only thing on her mind was the enormous and angry alligator she had in her trailer.

As she rode the hood of the Hummer, she flexed the muscles in her neck in anticipation and cracked her knuckles. She was ready.

84

SONNY BOY WAS READY TOO. HE HAD SPECIAL-ordered two dozen gold-plated shovels to use for the groundbreaking ceremony. They were all lined up on the veranda. He had had each one personalized with the name of a different dignitary.

"Party favors," he called them. After the ground breaking, everyone could take their engraved shovel home and have it mounted, to remind them of this monumental occasion.

But right away his glee turned to glum. Thinking about mounting made him remember the bird in the glass case. The ivory-billed woodpecker. Shot by his father, Quenton, who had ended up in the top of a tree, dead of a heart attack.

A shiver ran up Sonny Boy's right leg and into his gut. And he might have called the whole thing off right there. . . . It was early, there was still time to back out. . . . Decisions, decisions . . . Except that just then, he saw the headlights from the Hummer coming toward him, and even though he was somewhat blinded by the blue-tinted lights, he could tell that Jaeger was sitting on the hood again, riding the car like a rodeo horse.

To further emphasize the point, he heard her yell, "Yee-haw!" She must have caught a gator, he thought. And sure enough, he heard the beast thrashing inside the trailer. And from the sounds of the thrashes, he figured it must be a large one. When he saw the trailer rock from side to side, he knew it was a *very large* one.

There was no going back now. Soon, the guests would arrive, including the mayor and her husband. An alligator would be wrestled. Fried pies would be eaten. Ground would be broken. The Brayburns would get their eviction notice. Best of all, the Gator World Wrestling Arena and Theme Park would be built and the cash would start rolling in.

Everything was going according to plan. The mounted bird in the case was no concern of his. It was fire the torpedoes, full speed ahead.

85

Paradise Pies Café was operating at full speed too. It was all Chap and his mother could do to keep up. When Coyoteman Jim stopped in after his radio shift, they gave him an apron and put him to work filling coffee cups.

Once again, the cash piled up. Chap kept taking the bills to the back porch and dropping them into the boat. Even though they still had a long way to go before it was filled, he could see that they were making progress.

Chap looked down at the ones, fives, tens, and even a handful of twos. What had once seemed hopeless, was now seeming possible. In fact, seeing all that cash made him think that maybe, just maybe, he might also be able to find the Sugar Man. Hope swam like a fish right up into his chest.

As he turned to go back to the kitchen, he heard the phone ring. He could tell by his mother's voice that someone was placing an order. In fact, he could tell by her face that it was a *big* order.

"Pies for twenty-four?" she said. Chap looked at her. That was a lot of pies. He looked at the clock. It was almost noon. After the morning rush, the pie supply was low.

"At one p.m.?" she asked.

Closing time? One p.m. was closing time. They would be completely out of pies by then. Chap knew that. Could they make pies for twenty-four by one p.m.?

To answer his question . . . "Of course we can have pies for twenty-four at one p.m.," he heard his mother say. "Of course we can."

He looked at the counter. There were only a few pies left, and there were still a handful of customers coming through the door.

But the next thing he heard his mother say caught him completely off guard, "Thank you, Mr. Beaucoup. We'll have them ready."

Mr. Beaucoup? Sonny Boy?

As soon as Mom set the phone down, Chap asked, "Sonny Boy Beaucoup is coming here with twenty-three other people?"

That's when Coyoteman Jim stepped in. Rubbing his hands on the front of his apron, he said, "Didn't y'all hear the announcement about the groundbreaking ceremony?" Judging from the looks on their faces, he guessed not.

Chap let the news soak in. A ground breaking? But . . .

but . . . it was too soon. How could they fill up the boat in such a short time? The little fish of hope that Chap had just experienced swam right down the toilet.

In the same exact moment, the truth ran up and bit him: A groundbreaking ceremony meant that all their options were off the table.

Chap realized right then that Sonny Boy and Jaeger had simply been playing a cruel joke on them. All that work, all the bills he and his mom had set inside the boat? They had never even had a chance. Sonny Boy had never intended for his deal to be real. Even if they had stuffed the little pirogue to the very brim with cash, it would never have been enough. Not in the face of a sprawling extravaganza like the Gator World Wrestling Arena and Theme Park.

And for the first time ever, Chap felt something he had never felt before. Not once. Not ever. Not in his whole twelve years. He felt humiliated. How could he have let himself be duped by someone with such stupid, stupid socks?

His mother recovered first. "Pies for twenty-four," she said. Then she handed Chap an unopened bag of Community Coffee. "We're going to need more."

Reluctantly, he took the bag and turned toward the grinder. This was not what he wanted to do. The high pitch of the grinder grated on his nerves. He could feel his cheeks burn in the hot air of the kitchen. Even without taking a single sip of coffee, his mouth was filled with bitterness.

All at once, he wanted to be *anywhere* but in the kitchen of Paradise Pies Café making stupid coffee that had not inspired even one stupid hair on his chest. He especially did not want to be making coffee for such a stupid person as Sonny Boy Beaucoup.

He felt trapped.

And in that split second, the sound of the coffee grinder peeled away every inch of nerve coating in his brain, and he remembered: "The trap!" In the flurry of the morning's activity, he had forgotten to check the Havahart trap.

He yanked his apron over his head and ran through the back of the cabin, past the boat, and down the steps of the back porch. *Wham!* The screen door slammed behind him.

Sure enough. The trap had worked. But not in the way he had intended. There, in full hissing and spitting glory, was one very large, very angry . . . primeval possum.

"Great balls of fire!" Chap cried. (Okay, he didn't really say that, but we can't repeat his true words in polite company.)

From behind the wires of the cage, one of the swamp's nastiest denizens glared at Chap with its tiny little black eyes and very, very sharp teeth. Chap gingerly stood behind the

Havahart cage and slowly lifted the lid, whereupon the primeval possum lumbered out.

While he watched the possum disappear into the thick underbrush, even more humiliation dripped down Chap's neck, his chest, his waist, until it settled right smack in the middle of his gut.

Could this day get any worse?

86

THE DAY WAS NOT GOING VERY WELL FOR A VERY large alligator either. *WHOOMPH!* With one last fierce shove, Jaeger Stitch grabbed the side of the ten-foot-long reptile and flipped him onto his back.

The gator had been a worthy foe. All morning long she had teased it with her pointed stick by poking it through the bars of the trailer. It had responded with a fury of snaps and hisses.

And then, once all of the dignitaries had arrived and settled at their tables on the wide veranda, once lunch had been served, Jaeger Stitch opened the back of the trailer, and the huge beast leapt out into the open. She circled it with her pointed stick.

Each time she prodded it, the gator whipped its tail toward her in an attempt to catch her and sweep her into its enormous mouth. After spending all those hours cooped up in the trailer, after all those jabs and pokes, the animal was furious.

Time after time, it leapt toward Jaeger. But she was too quick for it. The folks on the veranda watched in amazement as the two feinted and dodged.

The alligator was a creature with a million years of survival instincts going for it. A species doesn't prowl the earth for such a long time without a surplus of skills to keep its kind going.

Jaeger Stitch was a creature of wile. After several minutes of provocation, Jaeger danced her way behind the alligator. Then with a running leap, she jumped onto its back, and with her tiny hands she reached for its foot-long jaws. The alligator's tail whipped furiously back and forth. At the same time, its mouth whipped back and forth too.

Jaeger held on.

What she knew, and what a lot of folks don't, is that an alligator has very little strength in opening its jaws. Where its power lies is in closing them.

Jaeger Stitch knew exactly what to do. First, she leaned forward until her cheek was almost between the beast's eyes. She pushed her face down hard against the alligator's face so that its jaws were forced to close, and then she clamped them shut with both of her hands. Once the alligator's jaws were clamped, the gator was powerless.

The wrestlerette slowly sat up, and as she did, she pulled the animal's head toward hers in a ninety-degree angle so that the alligator's snout was facing straight up toward the sky. She held it there for a long minute, and right before she let her hands go, she leaned forward and kissed it.

She kissed the alligator.

And as soon as she did, she leapt off its back, spun around on her toes, and bowed to the audience. They all stood up and gave her a rousing ovation. None of them had ever seen anything quite like it. Sonny Boy's smile went from ear to ear. It was obvious that they were all in the presence of the World Champion Gator Wrestler of the Northern Hemisphere. Suddenly, they all knew what Sonny Boy knew: People would come from miles around to see her. The economy of the region was about to pick up. The mayor even shook Sonny Boy's hand.

Right on cue, Leroy pulled the superstretch Hummer up the drive. "Grab your shovels, everyone," said Sonny Boy. And the entire group, all twenty-four of them, plus Leroy, headed to Paradise Pies Café for pre-groundbreaking dessert.

As for the alligator, once it managed to roll itself back onto its legs, it headed for the azaleas, where it took a nice, long nap.

87

OKAY, YOU WANT TO TALK ABOUT NAPS? THE SUGAR Man had been napping for a very long time, and even though there was an emergency at hand, he moved rather slowly, know what I mean? Waking up was hard to do. He scooped up Bingo and J'miah in one of his palmetto-size hands and set them on his shoulder.

To Bingo it was almost like being at the top of a tree. He loved it.

To J'miah it was almost like being at the top of a tree too. Frankly, he didn't feel the love at all.

Both of them grabbed fistfuls of fur in order to hang on.

Raccoons are quite dexterous. They can swim, climb, and scamper better than most other critters. (One mode of transportation that they don't do is flight, and that can be excused for lack of wingage.) But riding atop the Sugar Man was a wholly new form of transportation. And even though J'miah had mixed emotions, it was much more expedient than trekking by foot through the dark trails of the forest.

"Let's go," Bingo urged.

And with that, the Sugar Man began to plod his way along, toward the Bayou Tourterelle and the canebrake sugar. Bingo and J'miah looked down at Gertrude, slithering ahead of them in the water. She was, in fact, a monster of a rattle-snake. But from their vantage points she didn't look nearly so menacing.

What was menacing was the *rumble-rumble-rumble-rumble*.

"Hurry," Bingo said.

"Hurry," J'miah said.

To our little Scouts, looking around at the beautiful green trees, with their wispy beards of moss, seeing the silvery bayou as it slowly slid to the sea, breathing in the thick, moist air of early summer, it seemed like the whole world was depending upon them.

"Hurry up," they said. "Hurry."

THERE WAS PLENTY OF HURRY-UP GOING ON AT
Paradise Pies Café. Chap stuffed sugarcane into the
juicer as fast as he could. Mom rolled out the batter. And
Coyoteman Jim washed the coffee cups. The deep-fat fryer
bubbled with pies.

Sweetums was in a hurry too. "Heads up, people!" he
said. But before he could really process his family's failures
of comprehension . . . *rumble, rumble, rumble, rumble* . . . he
scrambled for his place underneath Chap's bed. The floorboards shook. The bed above him shook. What if the bed
fell on top of him? He shot out from under there. But the
open room was too . . . open.

The closet!

He darted into the farthest corner and curled into a
very tight ginger ball. He had done what he could.

Rumble-rumble-rumble-rumble.

89

In the café, the last of the regular customers had just rolled away when Chap looked through the kitchen window and saw the Hummer roll in. Like it had before, it took up the entire parking lot and then some.

As Chap watched, the driver hurried to the side doors and swung them open. Twenty-four people, including Sonny Boy and Jaeger, stepped onto the red gravel surface. Chap could see that all of them were dressed in fancy suits and shiny shoes; the mayor and her husband even wore matching scarves. None of their outfits were suitable for mucking about in the swamp. In their hands each of them held a gold-plated shovel. Chap watched as one by one the dignitaries leaned their shovels against the porch rail.

"Guess they're gonna eat pies first, then do the ceremony," said Coyoteman Jim. Chap could tell that was right. The golden shovels gleamed in the afternoon sun.

"Pies for everyone," ordered Sonny Boy Beaucoup as they filed in through the door. In the kitchen, the sound of Sonny Boy's voice scraped against Chap's insides. The knot of humiliation that had smacked him earlier reared back and smacked him again. Whatever manliness he had acquired over the past few days flew right out the window. Worst of all, Chap now knew exactly what it meant to "be put in one's place."

Face it, old Chap, he thought. You lost.

But as he waited for the twenty-four dignitaries to take their seats, he made a decision. He might have lost, but he was not a loser. He was *not* going to let Sonny Boy Beaucoup, with his stupid socks, know that he, Audie Brayburn's grandson, had been bested. His mind raced over the image of the greater roadrunner his grandfather had drawn in the sketchbook, the one with the heart drawn over its breast. It rested on the word "greater." "Greater Chaparral." That's what it said. Not "greater roadrunner." Not "lesser roadrunner." Greater Chaparral.

And with that in mind, he straightened into his full six-foot-plus frame. He might be a boy, but he was a tall boy. Taller than Sonny Boy. Taller than Jaeger Stitch. Taller even than the mayor and her husband.

Like trees. Grandpa's voice whispered in his ear.

With that, Chap walked out of the kitchen with a heaping tray of fresh, hot fried sugar pies and started serving them up. As soon as the dignitaries got a whiff of them, they dug in. All you could hear was chewing and chomping. The smell of sugar filled the air.

Finally, the mayor said, "My, those were wonderful." She wiped her mouth with her napkin and grinned. That was followed by many, many compliments. When everyone was finished, Sonny Boy tried to hand Chap a stack of bills. "Here," he said, "this should cover it."

Chap looked at the stack. He could see that it was way more money than was called for. "I threw in a little tip," Sonny Boy said. Then he started laughing his ridiculous laugh. Chap was used to tips. Most of their customers left tips. But this was more than a tip. It was something else. It was pity. Sonny Boy thrust it at him again. "Here, boy," he said. But Chap just stood there. He wanted nothing to do with Sonny Boy's money or his pity.

And even though there were more than two dozen people in the same room with him, Chap felt more alone than ever. The cloud of lonesome that his grandpa had left behind sat right between his shoulder blades.

While Chap stood there, staring at the wad of cash in Sonny Boy's outstretched hand, Chap's mother walked up. He would let her handle the money. But instead of reaching out for it, she put a dab of flour on Chap's cheek. And in that simple gesture, Chap felt the smallest bit of courage.

"Keep it," he told Sonny Boy. "It's on the house."

90

THEY SAY THAT LIGHTNING NEVER STRIKES IN THE same place twice, but the same is not true for courage. As it turns out, when courage strikes, it almost always begets more courage.

"Whatever," said Sonny Boy, staring at Chap, who suddenly seemed way too tall to be a twelve-year-old boy. Sonny Boy tucked the wad of bills back into his pocket. Then he and Jaeger led the rest of the groundbreaking contingency out the front door. One by one they collected their gold-plated shovels.

While they were doing that, Chap Brayburn, filled with twice-struck courage, rushed to the back porch. He swung open the door and hauled the pirogue, now two-thirds filled with cash, down the steps and into the yard. The groundbreakers would have to walk right by it, and sure enough there they came.

Chap blurted out to Sonny Boy, "Here you go, Mr.

Beaucoup. As long as you're taking cash, you might as well take a boatload."

Sonny Boy stopped in his tracks. Chap could tell that he had not expected that. So he added, "It was a deal, remember?" Sonny Boy tried to ignore Chap. He looked over his shoulder. He brushed the front part of his seersucker suit and straightened his tie. Then he waved for the shovelers to press ahead.

But first, the mayor chimed in, "You made a deal with this young man? What deal?" By then Chap's mother and Coyoteman Jim had caught up with the crowd.

Chap could see that Sonny Boy felt cornered. His jaw tightened. He clenched his teeth. His freckles popped out against the skin of his pale cheeks. Jaeger stepped up next to him. Her eyes blazed.

Chap spoke up, "A deal—a boatload of cash." He didn't mention the Sugar Man.

"That's exactly what you said," added his mother. She walked up next to Chap.

"Sure I did," said Sonny Boy, trying to get his jaw loose enough to smile. Then he pointed to the pirogue. "But surely you don't call *that* a boat?" He paused. "When I said a 'boat,' I meant something along the lines of a yacht." All at once, Chap realized how small the little pirogue was, only large enough for two, himself and his grandfather.

Somehow the bills that rested inside it looked pathetic.

And with that, Sonny Boy said, "Does anybody see a *boat* here?"

"I don't see a boat," said one of the dignitaries.

"Boat?"

"Is that a boat?"

"Rather picayune, if you ask me."

Picayune? What does that even mean?

Then, to Chap's disbelief, Sonny Boy took his toe and turned the pirogue onto its side. The small bills that had been set in there so lovingly by Chap and his mother and Coyoteman Jim, set there with so much hope, went floating out into the afternoon air. Some of them flew into the trees, some of them wafted into the pricker vines and stuck there. Most of them just sat beside the boat in a modest heap.

"Oops," said Sonny Boy. (We believe that is the third "oops" we've heard recently.) As if that weren't bad enough, Sonny Boy said, "I don't suppose you've seen the Sugar Man, too?" Sonny Boy's laughter rolled over Chap's crushed heart. And if that wasn't bad enough, Jaeger stepped in with her own brand of humor. "I don't suppose pigs fly," she said, whereupon another gale of laughter engulfed the group.

Chap wanted to spit on Jaeger Stitch, but then he decided that he didn't want to waste his good spit. Instead, he crossed his arms and spun around. He couldn't look at them anymore, couldn't look at his grandfather's boat, lying on its side.

Chap closed his eyes as tight as he could to keep the hot, furious tears from rolling down his cheeks. Finally, he opened them again and turned back toward the bayou. He could see the backs of the groundbreakers as they marched in a single line toward the canebrake. With their gold-plated shovels over their shoulders, they looked like horrid little trolls, going to dig a hole that would drain the entire swamp.

Chap felt like he was caught in their hideous whirlpool. To keep from being sucked under, he sat down hard, right on the ground, and dropped his burning face into his hands.

But then he had a horrible thought: The groundbreakers were on the trail to the canebrake. With his heart pounding in his chest, he realized, *Oh no!* Each one of the dignitaries was a walking, talking target for . . . *Crotalus horridus.* Canebrake rattlers.

He might have hated all of those gold-plated shovelers, but he was still . . . "Wait!" he called. "Wait!" He ran after them.

But instead of heeding his pleas, Sonny Boy turned around and snapped at him. "Haven't we had enough out of you, kid?"

"Snakes!" said Chap.

But the marchers just kept on marching.

91

IN THE DEEPEST, DARKEST RECESSES OF CHAP'S CLOSET, Sweetums curled his ginger body into a ginger ball. The *rumble-rumble-rumble-rumble*s were making him shed. He was a sorry sight.

92

FOR AN EVEN SORRIER SIGHT, TAKE A LOOK AT SONNY Boy Beaucoup's socks. As he walked down the trail behind his merry band, Jaeger in the lead, his socks kept getting snagged on the pricker vines, which seemed to reach for them. Step. Snag. Step. Snag.

He finally leaned down to pull one of the burrs out. "Ouch!" The points were sharp. They poked into his fingertips.

Then he stumbled over another pricker vine. He reached for it. "Ouch!" A drop of blood pooled on his fingertip. For a moment he felt a little woozy. He had never been very good at the sight of blood, especially his own.

But this blood was even worse because it reminded him of the bloody deal that sat on the family mantel. Chiding the boy about the Sugar Man had unnerved him more than he wanted to admit. What if . . . The words of his great-great-greater-greatest-grandfather's deal seared into his sight: "risk *the wrath of the Sugar Man*." Then his own words rose into his ears . . . *If I see some proof of the Sugar Man, I'll give you the whole darned swamp.*

He started to stick his fingers into his mouth, but thought better of it and pulled out his silk handkerchief. After all, he had plenty of them. He could spare this one. Once he stanched the bleeding, he let the handkerchief fall to the ground. He wouldn't miss it. Nor would he miss this swamp, especially when it became the Gator World Wrestling Arena and Theme Park. Who would?

"Nobody who matters," he said out loud. With that, he made a promise to himself. As soon as he returned to the Homestead, he would burn that freaking document, and for good measure he would toss in the mounted woodpecker specimen along with it. Enough with the past. It was time to look forward.

It was also time to look ahead. As in *down* the trail. Because if he had, he would have seen why the entire group of twenty-three shovelers suddenly turned around and ran *up* the trail, straight toward him, screaming bloody murder.

"Snakes!"

"Rattlesnakes!"

"They're everywhere!"

"Run for your lives!"

Sure enough, Jaeger Stitch and her groupies had come

face-to-face with a buzzing, writhing, hissing hive of *Crotalus horridus*—in the hundreds. Make that *thousands*. Okay, *tens of thousands*! Including one CHG—Gertrude!

Chichichichi!

93

AND THAT'S THE WARNING THAT THE UNFORTUNATE
hogs did not receive, coming as they were from the oppo-
site direction, because only minutes later they saw that
wild muscovado sugar, and hallelujah, pass the gravy, they
dug in. But it wouldn't have mattered if they had gotten
the message, because snakes were no concern of theirs.

In their sugar haze, they rooted and tooted. They snorted
and squealed. They gobbled and gorged.

"WWWHHHEEEEEEEE...OOOOOOHHHHHH...
WWWWHHHHEEEEEEE...OOOHHHHHHH...
WWWWWHHHHEEEEE...OOOOHHHH."

Those hogs noshed until the hogs came home. (Sorry,
couldn't resist.) They tore through that cane, ripping it out
of the ground and tramping it and stamping it and mostly,
hogging it. They paid no attention to the startled rattlesnakes, who slithered into the deepest end of the bayou,
where they shivered so hard that they stirred the water up
and made it look like chocolate soup.

Even Gertrude was too rattled to rattle. She quickly wound her enormous body around the trunk of a sturdy pine tree and shivered.

So, you can just imagine how mad the Sugar Man was when he saw those hogs rampaging through his wild sugarcane. First, he lifted Bingo and J'miah off his shoulders and set them on the branches of the same pine tree that Gertrude had embraced. They clung for dear life. Then, it's safe to say, that Sugar Man went wild. Hog wild.

He reached for the biggest of the batch, which just happened to be Buzzie, and with one hand the Sugar Man grabbed that hog's back leg and swung him around and around in a huge circle. He looked like a helicopter with a big fat bristly blade.

"Clyyyyydddiiiine!" yelled Buzzie, just before the Sugar Man let loose. Oh boy, did he let loose. That hog flew. Yep, you heard it, he flew through the hot, humid air of the swamp, way above the trees, up into the gathering clouds and straight toward the planets, like a big fat comet with a little curly tail.

He was followed by Clydine, who was trailed by all fifteen of their airborne progeny. If you looked straight up, it would seem like a porcine meteor shower, that's how high the Sugar Man tossed them.

94

IN THE PARKING LOT, THE NON-GROUNDBREAKERS had shoved their ways into the stretch Hummer. With Jaeger in the lead, and Sonny Boy bringing up the rear, everyone was stumbling and bumbling and swinging their shovels. It was a flat-out miracle that they didn't whack one another, because clearly these were people who had no idea how to swing a shovel.

The undignified dignitaries scrambled into the car. Then poor Leroy had to swing the doors shut and hurry to the driver's seat.

Hummers were originally built for warfare. That was their design, their calling. But this one had been all glammed up. And I'll tell you, it seemed like its sense of purpose was lost in the glamming. Some things are best left alone, if you know what I mean. Hummers should be out in the desert, tracking down enemies. Not hauling around citified groundbreakers with their picayune gold-plated shovels.

The Hummer was literally stuck in neutral. It couldn't move at all.

"Go!" cried Sonny Boy to Leroy. But when Leroy stepped on the gas, the wheels just spun in their deep tracks. Finally, Jaeger got out and kicked it from behind. Maybe it just needed its booty kicked? Who knows?

Leroy finally got it into gear, and good riddance is what we say.

95

DID ANY OF THOSE DIGNITARIES SEE THE HOGS BEING launched into the heavens? Did even one of them spy the Sugar Man in all his wrathful glory? Was there a single witness in the entire gold-plated bunch?

Friends, we are sorry to say, there was not.

96

But what about Chap?

While everyone else, including his mother and Coyote-man Jim, ran in the other direction, Chap headed as fast as he could toward the canebrake. He started singing the lullaby as loud as his voice would carry, hoping to calm those rattlers down.

When he got to the ruined canebrake, he came to a screeching halt. There, right on the water's edge, stood a man with hands the size of palmetto ferns. His hair looked just like the Spanish moss that hung on the north side of the cypress groves, and the rest of his body was covered in rough black fur, like the fur of the *ursus americanus luteolus*, UAL, that had only recently returned to the region after a very long absence.

Beside him, in a huge coil, Gertrude rattled her gigantic rattle. *Chichichichi.* Chap froze. *Crotalus horridus GIGAN-TICUS.* CHG. He watched as the Sugar Man patted her on the head, and then the Sugar Man looked directly at Chap.

Something about the boy reminded him of someone. Someone he had met long ago. Someone he counted as a friend. Someone he missed.

And then he remembered: Audie Brayburn. "Ahh," he said to Chap. "You're his grandson."

Chap nodded, and as he did, the Sugar Man looked directly at him and said these remarkable words: *"Nosotros somos paisanos."*

We are fellow countrymen. We are of the same soil.

And just like that, the cloud of lonesome that had hovered over Chap all these days grew a little lighter.

97

THE SUGAR MAN. CHAP. TWO NEW FRIENDS. BOTH of whom had loved Audie. Both of whom loved the swamp. No other words were needed between them.

After the Sugar Man watched Chap walk away, he sat down on the banks of the Bayou Tourterelle and grabbed himself a couple of fistfuls of wild cane sugar. It was just as good as he remembered. He surveyed the damage.

The hogs had definitely wreaked some havoc, but cane grew fast. He could see that it would recover.

"That's some mighty good sugarcane," he said to Gertrude. Gertrude just wrapped herself up in one big coil. A gigantic yawn came out of her mouth. And you know what happens when someone yawns? It makes everyone yawn.

Pretty soon the Sugar Man was yawning and yawning. "I believe I'll take a nap now," he said to Gertrude.

And then he looked at Bingo and J'miah, still clinging to the branches of the pine tree. He scooped them up in his palmetto-size hand and set them on the dry banks.

"Well done, Swamp Scouts," he said.

Bingo and J'miah beamed. Bingo felt so proud that even his tuft sat down. J'miah didn't squint at all. Both of them stood as tall as they could on their back paws, and with their front paws they saluted.

"I believe the emergenssssssie isss over," said Gertrude. And together she and the Sugar Man turned away from the banks of the Bayou Tourterelle and respectively slithered and strode back to their cozy lair. It's dark there, and quiet. A good place for snoozing, and dreaming, and for the Sugar Man to get some rest. After all, he's as old as the swamp itself.

The Last Night

98

BINGO AND J'MIAH WAVED GOOD-BYE TO GERTRUDE
and the Sugar Man. Then they meandered back to the
DeSoto. They took their own sweet time. After the rush of
the past few days, it felt nice to stroll through their nighttime neighborhood, especially now that the hideous hogs
were just a footnote in history.

By the time they got back to Information Headquarters,
it was late, and even though raccoons, as we said, were nocturnal, Bingo announced, "I'm going to take a nap." J'miah
was tired too, but he wasn't quite ready to sleep. He was too
full of the good energy that came from successfully complet-
ing their mission. He glanced at the art on the dashboard—
there it stood, the photo of the armadillo.

He sat back and admired it. He also admired the music
thingie. Then he wondered if maybe there was some other
treasure in the box under the seat. All at once, he wasn't
tired at all. He stuck his paw into the dark opening and
tapped around and around with his extra sensitive fingers.

He patted and patted and patted. It seemed like the box

might be empty. He gave it another pat. Nothing. But before he gave up, he reached as far back as he could, all the way up to his armpit.

Pat pat pat. He extended his fingers, right to the very farthest end of the box. And there, way at the back, he felt something. Something papery and thin, but stiff too. He patted some more. Wait a minute. He felt two somethings.

"Bingo!" he said. (Don't you love it when he does that?)

He pulled the somethings out. In his paw he held two more square pieces of art. One by one, he held them up and squinted his eyes so that he could focus on them. Then, he couldn't resist, he tapped his brother on the shoulder and showed them to him.

"Look!" said J'miah, holding up the first. He leaned over the backseat and held it right in Bingo's face.

"What is it?" asked Bingo.

"It's a bird," said J'miah, holding the paper up between them.

"I wonder what kind of bird it is," said Bingo. It wasn't any sort of bird that he had ever seen here in the swamp. He watched as J'miah set it next to the armadillo on the dashboard, and then to his surprise J'miah said, "Wait, there's another one."

Bingo rubbed his eyes. He stared at the picture; a furry face stared back at him. Then he smiled. "That's the best one of all," he said. J'miah agreed. And he propped it up next to the other two on the front dashboard.

"Perfect," Bingo said. The three pictures were perfect. But when J'miah looked around, the DeSoto did not look perfect. It looked dusty. Mission Clean-Up Headquarters picked up where it left off, and J'miah went into a cleaning frenzy.

He rubbed the inside of the windows. He dusted the dashboard. He swept the seats. Finally, Bingo couldn't take it anymore. J'miah needed an intervention.

"J'miah," he said, "now that you're not afraid of heights . . ."

J'miah leaned back. It was true, he had, in fact, climbed that magnolia tree. He had also ridden on the shoulders of the Sugar Man. And he perched on the upper branches of a pine tree while the Sugar Man dispatched the hogs. In none of those instances had he thrown up.

"What are we waiting for?" J'miah asked, and together the two of them slipped out of the entryway and into the welcoming night. As they strode away, J'miah stopped. "I just have to do one thing," he said. And while Bingo waited, J'miah took a large leaf, climbed onto the hood of the DeSoto, and dusted off the bust of the old conquistador. "That's been bothering me," he said, admiring his handiwork.

"Come on," said Bingo, and he pulled his brother all the

way to the edge of the bayou to the longleaf pine. Together, they climbed and climbed and climbed, all the way to the very top. And of course, once they were there, Bingo said, "Look!"

J'miah looked up. There were billions and trillions of stars. There was the whole Milky Way. And there, blinking like crazy, was a red star. He'd never seen anything like it.

"Meet Blinkle," said Bingo.

"Blinkle?" asked J'miah.

Bingo nodded. Then he said, "Make a wish."

"A wish?" asked J'miah.

"Of course," said Bingo. "That's what stars are for."

And if you think that Bingo and J'miah wished for a new mission, well, you would be correct: Operation Pie Procurement.

They scooted down that longleaf pine and headed straight for the café. It didn't take them long, but when they arrived, the café was shuttered. That was a good thing. They needed to strike while the dark was still covering them.

But hold on!

"Is that what I think it is?" asked Bingo.

"Havahart," said J'miah.

Sure enough the Havahart trap sat directly beneath the kitchen window. They couldn't see that it was not set. All they could see was its menacing wires. Scouts knew all about Havahart traps. Plenty of their unwitting relatives had been trapped and relocated.

Bingo stood back from the house and took a long view. "Oh well," he said. Then he smiled. "I could use a crawdad!"

J'miah grinned. "Me too."

But instead of turning around and loping down to Crawdad Lane, they both kept looking at the café. It was hard to give up that wish. The problem was, they waited just one moment too long, because while they were sitting there, someone inside the house flipped on a switch and flooded the yard with light.

Bingo and J'miah froze. Their cover was blown. They should run. They should turn around and skedaddle. Which they did. They skedaddled right for Crawdad Lane.

The Last Day

99

As for Chaparral Brayburn, he was wide awake. He'd been wide awake all night. He now knew for certain that the Sugar Man was still extant. (There's that word again.) But he was the only one who had seen him. And did he have a camera with him at the time?

Of course not.

After the Hummer had screamed out of the parking lot, leaving huge ruts in its wake, Chap and his mom, with the help of Coyoteman Jim, had spent the rest of the afternoon picking every last bill out of the pricker vines. So far, he had not told his mom about the meeting with the Sugar Man. He didn't quite know how to share it yet. And besides, he still had no proof, did he?

Chap knew that after the debacle with the ground breaking, it was highly unlikely that Sonny Boy would try to build the Gator World Wrestling Arena and Theme Park. Once word got out about the plethora of rattlesnakes, no one would want to venture into the area again, even if it was paved with acres and acres of concrete.

But he also knew that as long as Sonny Boy was in charge of the swamp, he'd come up with something else just as worrisome, maybe something worse, if that was even possible.

There was only one recourse: Chap would have to try to follow the Sugar Man's tracks to his lair and take his picture. Of course, this was a plan that might work if he only had a camera. Grandpa Audie had never found or replaced the Polaroid. And even if he had the prized Land Camera, there was no film for it.

Think, Chap, think.

Think think think.

He looked around the room, even though he knew there was no camera. He checked beneath his bed. Nothing. He opened his closet door. Sweetums. Then he walked to his desk. There it sat. His grandfather's old sketchbook. He carried it from his desk and set it on his bed. Then he pulled it toward his face. There was his grandpa's smell—sugar and bullfrogs and red dirt.

The book fell open in his lap, right to the blank white page, the one where the woodpecker should rightfully be. A familiar heat scratched the back of his throat. So long as Sonny Boy and his ilk were around, the woodpecker would never have a chance. Chap knew this. He swallowed. His throat burned.

He flipped the pages, and there was the drawing of the Sugar Man his grandpa had made. Chap was surprised at how well his grandfather had captured him. For a brief moment, he thought that maybe he could draw his own picture of the furry guy.

But in an even briefer moment, he thought, No. That wouldn't prove anything.

He closed the book and set it beside him on the bed. The numbers on his clock glared at him. Three o'clock in the morning. And not a wink of sleep. And on top of that, his mother would be rising in another hour to get ready for another day of pies. He should be dead-tired, but instead he felt *wired for sound*, as his mom would say.

He needed to figure out how to prove that the Sugar Man existed. But how?

He looked all around. Nothing.

Nothing nothing nothing.

He was completely bereft of good ideas.

Then . . . he remembered . . . Steve! Steve's cell phone. Unless Steve had popped in during one of the pie rushes, the cell phone should still be on the windowsill beside the radio.

Chap stepped down the hall and into the kitchen.

"Please-be-there-please-be-there-please-be-there," he chanted.

Yes! There it was. Chap pressed the button at the bottom of the screen. The screen lit right up. Then he pushed the icon for the camera, and it snapped open. Without one ounce of hesitation, Chap slipped the phone into his pocket and headed toward the door, pulling on his muck boots as he went. But before he opened the door, he stepped back into the kitchen and stuffed a couple of pies into his other pocket. They were left over and destined for the catfish anyways, but he didn't mind.

Might need some breakfast, he thought.

Next he reached for his flashlight, and finally he grabbed his machete. After all, there were pricker vines to consider.

As he opened the door, he flipped on the yard light and stepped outside. There and there, just a few steps away, sat the raccoons.

"Thieves," he said.

As soon as he said it, the pair vamoosed, disappeared into the woods. Like ghosts, thought Chap. Like ghosts.

100

FIRST, CHAP WALKED DOWN THE FAMILIAR TRAIL TO
the canebrake. He paused long enough to sing the rattlesnake lullaby. Even though he had no plans to chop cane
just then, he didn't need a chance encounter with the
snakes. Once there, he shined his flashlight all around.

Sure enough, he found plenty of tracks. There were the
obvious snake tracks. Plenty of those. He even saw his own
tracks, made by the same pair of muck boots that he had
on his feet just then. Once again he saw raccoon tracks.
Of course he saw some alligator tracks. But in all of the
muck, he only saw one discernible track that could have
been made by the Sugar Man. And even that was fuzzy. As
fuzzy as the Sugar Man himself.

Standing there behind the beam of his flashlight, he
wondered if he had really seen the big guy. Or had he
dreamed him? How, he wondered, could a creature so large
leave so little evidence? He scanned the banks of the Bayou

Tourterelle with his flashlight. Nothing. As far as he could see, the Sugar Man had not left any distinct tracks.

Chap's heart sank. Proof. There was no proof. Just a single fuzzy print. He reached into his pocket for the camera. He could at least take a photo of that. But when he pushed the button on the slick glass of the phone, nothing happened. He pushed it again. Nothing. The screen was as blank as could be.

"Jeepers creepers!" he said right out loud. (Okay, that's not really what he said, but it's close enough.) It had been days since Steve had forgotten his phone, and in all those days nobody had charged it up. How could they? Steve had the charger. Chap felt like throwing the phone into the bayou. And he might have, but then he remembered that it wasn't his to throw. He slipped it back into his pocket.

Defeated, Chap turned around. He might as well go back to the café now to help his mother start the pies, he thought. Without a camera, what was the point of finding the Sugar Man? The sky was turning deep blue. He knew his way without the flashlight, so he clicked it off. As soon as he did, with the silhouettes of the tall trees surrounding him, and the quiet hum of the swamp just waking up, he realized that he wasn't quite ready to go back.

He could stay out for a little while longer. But which way to go? East? West? North? South wasn't an option because that would lead him straight into the bayou. Unlike Jaeger Stitch, he had no desire to wrestle an alligator. So he licked his finger and held it up to the sky. There was a slight breeze coming from the west, so he turned in that direction.

He decided to stick to the banks of the bayou. The sky above the water offered a little bit more light than the darkness he would encounter in the thick woods.

He didn't go very far, however, before he came upon a small ditch. He barely caught sight of it in the growing light. If he had worn his waders, he might have just sloshed across it. So, instead he went around. He only took a few steps back toward the bayou when he realized that he was going uphill. If he had been paying close attention, that might have seemed a bit odd, but his thoughts had turned to the café again. He was going to have to head back soon to help his mother. Besides, he had not left a note for her, and he knew she'd be worried.

Plus, there were only a couple of hours before they would open the doors, and it took that long to set everything up.

He was just about to turn around when the baby sun splashed a ray onto something bright in the corner of his eye, something that glimmered. Probably a can, he thought. It made him downright mad the way trash floated up the bayou. But this splash of light did not seem like a can. And besides, it wasn't in the bayou. Then he realized that it also wasn't on the ground. Actually, it was lodged in a big thicket of brush.

A *big* thicket of brush.

Chap drew closer. But as he moved, his body blocked the sun's light and the object disappeared. He stepped to one side and waited. There it was again. He focused on the exact spot, and even though he couldn't see anything, he crept toward the thicket. All of his grandpa's years of teaching rose up inside of Chap. One step. Two steps. He took care to raise and lower his feet as quietly as he could.

Then he stopped. What if the glow he had seen was actually a reflection from a wild animal's eyes, caught momentarily in the sun's beams? He felt the warm handle of the machete in his hand. Three steps. Four steps.

He straightened up. Six feet plus. Surely no animal, aside from the Sugar Man, would match his height, would it? Five steps. Six steps. He moved forward toward the spot where he last saw the glimmer.

Seven steps. Eight steps. He gripped his machete in his right hand and took another step. His hand started to shake. To steady it, he gripped the heavy knife with both hands and gently, oh so gently, raised the blade to shoulder level and moved a vine. The light splashed right into his eyes.

He jumped back.

"Ooohhhhh," he cried. He rubbed his eyes and blinked. Could it be? Was it true? He could feel his heart pounding in his ears, his nose, his whole body. Staring right at him was a tiny face with a helmet. It was a chrome bust. Of a conquistador. Not just any conquistador. Hernando de Soto. Chap's heart went *kaPow kaPow* in his chest. He looked over his right shoulder. He looked over his left shoulder. He looked straight ahead. Then, he couldn't help it, he let go of the machete and raised his hands over his head and spun in a circle. He spun and spun and spun until he spun himself into a mad whirling dervish. He couldn't stop the crazy spinning of his whole six-foot-plus-some being. He didn't want to.

And while he spun, he called out, "Grandpa!" At the top of his voice, "Grandpa!"

The whole woods echoed with his cries.

"Grandpa!" bounced from one tree to another, skimmed atop the water in the Bayou Tourterelle, flew between the branches and vines. It even settled between the ears of the snoozing Sugar Man, who rolled over in his sleep and smiled.

Joy. Yes. Joy.

In that very moment of Chaparral Brayburn's young life, the name "Grandpa" was another name for "joy."

And Chap, grinning from ear to ear, finally stopped his

mad spin and with both hands reached right into the brush and pulled. Then he pulled again and again and again. He paid no attention to the stinging pricker vines that dug into his palms and stuck to his pants. He pulled and yanked and tugged, until at last, there it was.

In all of his trampings and stampings through the swamp with Grandpa Audie, he had never noticed it, that's how well it was hidden. He and his grandpa had probably walked right by it a thousand times without ever seeing it. They had surely drifted by it on the bayou and never noticed it from their pirogue. And yet, there it stood.

Chap walked around it. Then walked around it again. The only thing that shone was the hood ornament. The rest of the car, what he could see of it, was so rusty that it blended right into the red dirt underneath it. He pulled away the vines from the front grille and stood back.

He couldn't help it. He had the unmistakable feeling that it was smiling at him.

"The DeSoto," he said. Wonder settled over him. All of the stories that his grandpa had told him, the ones about taking the photograph of the ivory-billed woodpecker, the one about getting lost in the swamp and suddenly finding the DeSoto in the light cast off by a bolt of lightning, how it was warm and dry and the seats were just as comfortable as a soft bed, all flooded back to Chap.

Then there was the one about stumbling out onto the highway, where a kind stranger picked up a sick camper and took him to the hospital in Port Arthur, where it took him several months to recover from the flu, and by the time he returned, the car was gone.

"The DeSoto," Audie had said, "saved my life." And then his soft voice would trail off. "But I never could find it after that. No matter how many times I looked, I could never find it."

Chaparral Brayburn stepped forward then and rubbed his hand along the hood. Flakes of rust sifted onto the ground. He curled his hand into a fist and rubbed away the dust from the old windshield and peered inside, but in the dim light of morning, it was difficult to see. He pulled on the door handle of the driver's side. It was rusted shut, so he tried the passenger door. He pulled and pulled, and finally, after one extra-hard yank, the old door creaked open. Chap looked inside. He expected it to be filled with dust, but instead it was neat and tidy. He also saw that the glass on the inside of all the windows had been rubbed until it sparkled. Yep, it was nice and clean. Mostly. On the surface anyways.

Wait! Paw prints. Some critter'd been in here. He took a closer look at the seat, then he turned around and examined the back of the seat. He also noticed the hole in the floorboard, an entryway. There they were, the unmistakable tracks.

"Raccoons," he said. This was their home. He looked around again. It was dry and sheltered and cozy—perfect for raccoons. He couldn't help but wonder if the two raccoons he had seen in the yard lights just an hour ago were the same ones who lived here.

If they were, he reckoned . . . then they were probably also the same ones who had broken into the café. Robbers! But Chap's enormous feeling of joy over finding the car dashed all thoughts of anger. That same joy made him reach inside his pocket and pull out the pies. They were a little smushed and also a bit stale, but he didn't think the raccoons would mind. However, as he placed them on the dashboard, he saw something else, something unexpected: three thin squares of old paper. Three thin squares propped up against the windshield. He shook his head. It couldn't be. But there, right in front of him, was the old photograph of the armadillo, and the second, of the ivory-billed woodpecker, and one other.

He stared hard at the one of the bird; he examined it as carefully as he had ever done anything in his whole life. It was a little faded, but there was no mistaking what it was. He started to pick it up, but before he did, he stopped. The three photos were lined up in a neat row. Chap could tell that care had been taken. It was hard to believe, he knew, but it was apparent that someone, the raccoons, had purposefully placed the pictures on the dashboard in a way that seemed like . . . well . . . like art.

Then Chap thought, There were two raccoons and one of him. Three. It only seemed fair that each of them should own a photograph. As much as he loved the photo of the bird, it was the third photo that he needed most. He would leave the other two for the raccoons.

You might recall that Audie Brayburn, in his feverish state, snapped an accidental photo on his Polaroid Land Camera. A photo of a fuzzy face. Remember that?

What Chap held in his hand was the third photo, a photo of the Sugar Man.

Proof.

Holding it as gently as he could between his fingers, he stared at it. The photo was as clear as it was the night his grandfather had snapped it more than sixty years before. It was just as lovely as it had been when Audie had slipped it into the .30-caliber ammo can, where it had remained in this old car. The DeSoto. His grandpa's beautiful car. It had saved his life.

And now? It could save the whole darned swamp.

101

Without Sonny Boy's support, Jaeger Stitch had no reason to stick around. Instead, she yanked her alligator out of the azaleas by its tail, hitched her trailer to a passing eighteen-wheeler, and headed for South America. We've heard that she is dazzling folks in the alligator-wrestling world and is quickly rising to become World Champion Gator Wrestler of the Southern Hemisphere. We wish her well. And the alligator, too.

As for Sonny Boy, once he got back to the Homestead, he made Leroy start a big bonfire. As soon as the chauffeur got the blaze to roar, Sonny Boy threw in the bloody deal made and signed by Alouicious, and then he tossed the specimen of the woodpecker on top of it and watched as it burned to a crisp.

But while he stood there, watching Leroy stoke the flames, he heard a very loud KABOOM.

"What was that?" asked Leroy, but before the echo from the first KABOOM stopped ringing, it was followed by another equally loud KABOOM, pursued by fifteen smaller but equally as startling KABOOMs.

It seems, junior birdmen, that whatever goes up must come down. Yep, once our hogs hit the outermost apogee of their stellar orbit, they reentered Earth's gravitational field and crashed right through the porch roof of the old Homestead.

That was it for Leroy. "Pigs are flying!" he cried. And for the second time in less than twenty-four hours, he hopped into the Hummer and peeled out down the road.

Every cell in Sonny Boy's body hummed. He pulled his socks up and started to shake. There wasn't a single hair on his yellow-gray head that wasn't sticking straight out. Nobody had to tell him who'd tossed those pigs into the sky. A creature full of wrath. The Sugar Man. A quick image of Sonny Boy's father, Quenton, dead in the top of a tree, blazed through his brain. And his brain told him, "If you don't get out of this swamp, a similar fate awaits you." The proof was in the details, or rather the hogs' tails. Right then, he drew up a deal and signed it . . . in blood.

I, SONNY BOY BEAUCOUP,
TURN OVER THIS WHOLE DARNED
SWAMP TO CHAPARRAL BRAYBURN.
GOOD RIDDANCE.
SIGNED,
SONNY BOY BEAUCOUP

He nailed it to the front door, where someone would surely find it. And as if the swamp itself wanted to seal the deal, when Sonny Boy ran his hands through his hair, there, tucked just behind his right ear, was a beautiful black feather with a white tip.

Last we heard, Sonny Boy was living in a desert area, someplace like Phoenix. Do we care? Not a whit.

102

As for Buzzie and Clydine, word on the street is that as soon as they brushed themselves off from their trips to outer space, they gathered up their brood and high-tailed it to Arkansas, where they hired themselves out as mascots for some of the local high school football teams.

We've heard that none of them will ever again put one bite of sugar into their porky little mouths.

It's not out of the range of possibilities.

103

WE'RE ALMOST TO THE FINISH LINE, SPORTS FANS, SO hang in. When Bingo and J'miah, their bellies full of crawdads, wandered back to the DeSoto, rain was beginning to fall, so they scampered in through the entryway of the passenger side. They were pooped. It had been a long few days, and both of them were ready for a nice summer snooze.

As soon as they entered the car, they noticed three things.

First: "Breaking and entering," declared J'miah.

Quickly, he looked around to see if anything had been taken. He checked his beloved photos. He loved the surprised look on the armadillo's face. He was also glad to see the photo of the bird, even though it wasn't a bird he recognized. And still in its place stood the photo of the Sugar Man. All three photos were right where he had left them. Whew!

The second thing they noticed was the distinctly human smell in the air, which explained the breaking and entering.

But the third thing they noticed was the other smell—sugar pies! Sure enough, there they were, two sugar pies, resting on the dashboard.

The brothers looked at each other in surprise. Bingo started laughing.

"Blinkle!" he said. "Our wishes came true!"

104

Now, all is well in Radioland, so far as we know. The cane has grown back. The rattlers are just as spicy as ever. The armadillos are surprised. J'miah has learned a song or two on the Marine Band music thingie. He's no Snooky Pryor, but he's getting there. Sweetums has finally come out of the closet. Steve got his phone back. Once the porch was repaired, the Old Beaucoup Homestead was turned into the Museum of Natural Swamp History. And the pies kick booty.

As for the ivory-billed woodpecker, since those old trees were left to stand, and the Sugar Man Swamp is safe from marauding hogs and merciless Beaucoups, maybe that woodpecker will return someday and bring her family with her. We're hoping. Lord God, we are.

There is only one unanswered question . . . the one about the photo of the Sugar Man. The moment Chap saw it, he knew . . . it could save the swamp.

And it might have, even without the flying hogs. But

while Chap sat there in his grandpa's beloved car, staring at proof of the Sugar Man, he also realized that the photo could stir up that swarm of hornets that Audie had warned him about.

When word got out that the Sugar Man was still extant, the thrill-seekers would flock to the swamp. A gazillion rattlesnakes would not keep their kind away. Nothing would be safe from their ropes and axes and shotguns.

How, Chap asked, could he do that to his grandpa's swamp? Wait. How could he do it to *his* swamp? An image of the drawing his grandpa had made of the greater road-runner flashed into Chap's head. And when it did, he heard Audie's voice, *Nosotros somos, paisanos!*

Taking care not to bump the other two photos, Chap set the one of the Sugar Man back on the dashboard, right next to the sugar pies. Then he stepped out of the car and with his back, leaned against the door until it closed. He stretched his arms out wide and declared, "This is paradise." And with that, our man of the household walked away. It was, we can safely say, a very good idea.

Acknowledgments

OFTEN, WRITING A STORY FEELS LIKE A WADE THROUGH a swamp. I might still be mucking about were it not for the kind assistance of my fellow *paisanos*: Debbie Leland, Laini Bostian, Jeanette Ingold, Rebecca Kai Dotlich, Kimberly Willis Holt, Marion Dane Bauer, Janet Fox, Donna Cooner, Diane Linn, Rose Eder, and Dennis Foley.

Right in the middle of the deepest, darkest lair, my agent, Holly McGhee, sent me a heart when my heart was breaking.

My editor, Caitlyn Dlouhy, was never afraid to wrestle the alligators, even when they gathered in the margins and lurked between the lines.

Elizabeth Harper Neeld listened while I told her about the raccoons and the car and the radio before I even wrote a single word. She was the one who said I needed pies. Oh, yes, pies were needed.

Also needed were answers about Hummers, which Phil at LA Custom Coaches provided. Thank you, Phil.

For answers about the DeSoto automobile, Dave Duricy manages a website called DeSotoLand: duricy.com/~desoto/.

I am indebted to the late J. Frank Dobie, for his 1939 essay, "The Roadrunner in Fact and Folklore," for background on the chaparral. And for all things IBWO, no one writes more passionately than Phillip Hoose. His book, *The Race to Save the Lord God Bird*, has had an honorary place on our coffee table for years.

Gratitude goes to my sweet husband, Ken, who sat beside me while I read the whole thing through out loud and helped me catch a boatload of mistakes. Jeannie Ng, copy editor extraordinaire, helped me correct those mistakes. It's safe to say, she saved my bacon. My mom, Pat Childress, laughed just when I needed to hear some laughter.

My biggest thanks goes to Cynthia Leitich Smith, who sent me an e-mail that said simply, "Write something funny." At first, I didn't understand. But now I do.